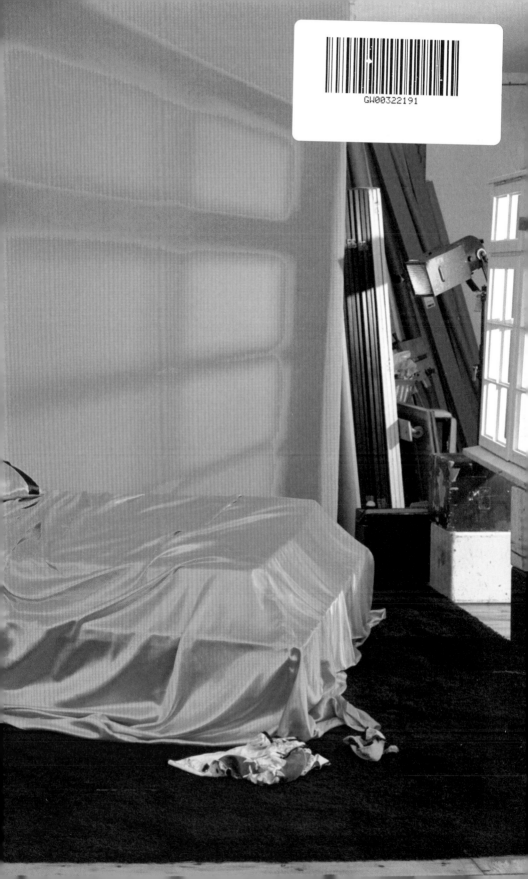

SNUFF

Chuck Palahniuk's eight novels are the bestselling *Rant*, *Haunted*, *Lullaby*, *Fight Club* – which was made into a film by director David Fincher – *Diary*, *Survivor*, *Invisible Monsters* and *Choke*. He is also the author of the non-fiction profile of Portland, Oregon, *Fugitives and Refugees*, and the non-fiction collection *Stranger Than Fiction*. He lives in the Pacific Northwest.

Also by Chuck Palahniuk

Fight Club
Survivor
Invisible Monsters
Choke
Lullaby
Fugitives and Refugees
Diary
Stranger Than Fiction
Haunted
Rant

CHUCK PALAHNIUK

JONATHAN CAPE · LONDON.

SNUFF

Published by Jonathan Cape 2008

1 3 5 7 9 10 8 6 4 2

Copyright © Chuck Palahniuk 2008

First published in Great Britain in 2008 by
Jonathan Cape
Random House, 20 Vauxhall Bridge Road,
London SW1V 2SA

www.rbooks.co.uk

Addresses for companies within The Random House Group Limited can be found at:
www.randomhouse.co.uk/offices.htm

The Random House Group Limited Reg. No. 954009

A CIP catalogue record for this book is available from the British Library

ISBN 9780224082464 (Hardback)
ISBN 9780224078580 (Trade Paperback)

The Random House Group Limited supports The Forest Stewardship
Council (FSC), the leading international forest certification organisation. All our
titles that are printed on Greenpeace approved FSC certified paper carry the FSC logo.
Our paper procurement policy can be found at
www.rbooks.co.uk/environment

Printed and bound in Great Britain by Clays Ltd, St Ives PLC

End papers: photograph © Jo Broughton

Duchess: Diamonds are of most value,
      They say, that have pass'd through
      most jewellers' hands.

Ferdinand: Whores, by that rule, are precious.

—John Webster, *The Duchess of Malfi* (I.ii)

SNUFF

1

Mr. 600

One dude stood all afternoon at the buffet wearing just his boxers, licking the orange dust off barbecued potato chips. Next to him, a dude was scooping into the onion dip and licking the dip off the chip. The same soggy chip, scoop after scoop. Dudes have a million ways of peeing on what they claim as just their own.

For craft services, we're talking two folding tables piled with open bags of store-brand corn chips and canned sodas. Dudes getting called back to do their bit—the wrangler announces their numbers, and these performers stroll back for their money shot still chewing a mouthful of caramel corn, their fingers burning with garlic salt and sticky with the frosting from maple bars.

Some one-shot dudes, they're just here to say they were. Us veterans, we're here for the face time and to do Cassie a favor. Help her one more dick toward that world record. To witness history.

On the buffet, they got laid out Tupperwares full of condoms next to Tupperwares of mini-pretzels. Fun-sized candy bars. Honey-roasted peanuts. On the floor, plastic wrappers from candy bars and condoms, bit and chewed open. The same hands scooping M&M's as reaching into the fly and elastic waistband of boxers to stroke their half-hard dicks. Candy-colored fingers. Tangy ranch-flavored erections.

Peanut breath. Root-beer breath. Barbecued-potato-chip breath getting panted into Cassie's face.

Tweakers scratching their arms bright red. High-school virgins wanting to lose it on camera. This one kid, Mr. 72, is looking to get deflowered and into history in the same shot.

Skinny dudes keeping their T-shirts on, shirts older than some other performers here, sent out for the launch of *Sex with the City* a lifetime ago. Fan-club shirts from back when Cassie was starring in *Lust Horizons*. T-shirts older than Mr. 72, silk-screened before he was born.

Loud dudes talk on cell phones, talking stock options and ground-floor opportunities at the same time they pinch and milk their foreskins. All the performers, the wrangler Magic Marker—ed their biceps with a number between one and six hundred. Their haircuts, a monument to gel and patience. Tans and fogs of cologne.

The room full of metal folding chairs. To set the mood, dog-eared skin magazines.

The talent wrangler is some babe, Sheila, with a clipboard, yelling for number 16, number 31, and number 211 to follow her up the stairway to the set.

2

Dudes wearing tennis shoes. Top-Siders. Bikini briefs. Wingtips with navy-blue calf-high socks held up with those old-time garters. Beach flip-flops still coated with sand, every step gritty with it.

That old joke: The way to get a babe to act in a blue movie is you offer her a million dollars. The way to get a dude is you just have to ask him . . . That's not actually a joke. Not like a ha-ha joke.

Except maybe us industry regulars, most of these no-bodies saw the ad that ran in the back of *Adult Video News*. An open casting call. A hard-on and a doctor's release to show you're clean, that was the audition. That, and nobody's shooting kiddie porn, so you had to be eighteen.

We got shaved pecs and waxed pubes standing in line with a Downs-syndrome softball team.

Asian, black, and spic dudes. A wheelchair dude. Something for every market segment.

The kid, dude 72, he's holding a bouquet of white roses starting to curl, droop, the petals slack and starting to brown. The kid's holding out one hand, words written on the back in blue ballpoint pen. Looking at them, the kid goes, "I don't want anything, but I've always loved you . . ."

Other dudes carry around wrapped boxes fluffy with bows and trailing ribbons, boxes small enough to fit in one hand, almost hidden inside their fingers.

The veteran talent wear satin bathrobes, prizefighter robes tied with a sash, while they wait their call. Professional woodsmen. Half them even dated Cassie, talked marriage, becoming the Lunts, the Desi and Lucy of adult entertainment.

Wasn't a performer at that shoot who didn't love Cassie Wright and want to help her make history.

Other dudes ain't dicked anything but their hand, watching nothing but Cassie Wright videos. To them, it's a kind-of fidelity. A marriage. These dudes, clutching their little gifts, for them today is their kind-of honeymoon. Consummation.

Today, her last performance. The opposite of a maiden voyage. Up those stairs, to anybody after the fiftieth dude, Cassie Wright will look like a missile crater greased with Vaseline. Flesh and blood, but like something's exploded inside her.

To look at us, you'd never guess we were making history. The record to end all records.

The talent wrangler comes around, calling out, "Gentlemen." The Sheila babe pushes the glasses up her nose and goes, "When I call you, you'll need to be camera-ready."

By that she means fully erect. Condom-ready.

The closest thing that comes to how the day felt is when you wipe back to front. You're on the toilet. You're not thinking, and you smear shit on the back of your hanging-down wrinkled ball skin. The more you try to wipe it clean, the skin stretches and the mess keeps getting bigger. The thin layer of shit spreads into the hair and down your thighs. That's how a day like this, how it feels to keep secret.

Six hundred dudes. One porn queen. A world record for the ages. A must-have movie for every discerning collector of things erotic.

Didn't one of us on purpose set out to make a snuff movie.

2

Mr. 72

It was a lamebrain plan, bringing roses. I don't know. The first step inside the door, they give you a brown paper shopping bag with a number written on the side, some number between one and six hundred. They say, "Put your clothes in here, kid." And they give you a wood clothespin with the same number in black pen. They say, "Clip it to your shorts. Don't lose it or you won't get your stuff back." The crew girl, she wears a stopwatch on a cord, hanging on her chest where her heart would be.

Taped to the wall behind the table where you undress, they got a sign done in the same black pen, on brown paper; it says how the production company isn't responsible for anybody's valuables.

Another sign they got says "No Masks Allowed."

Some bags, guys put their shoes in with a sock balled inside each. Their belt coiled tight and nested in one shoe. Their pants folded, the creases matched, and laid

5

on top the shoes. Their shirts tucked under their chin while they match up the arms and fold the collar and tails so as to make the least wrinkles. Their undershirt, folded. Their necktie rolled and tucked in a pocket of their suit jacket. Guys with good clothes.

Other guys pull off their jeans or sweatpants, balled up, inside out. Their T-shirts or sweatshirts. They peel off their damp underwear, and stuff it into the bags, then on top they drop their stinking tennis shoes.

After you undress, the stopwatch girl takes your bag of clothes and puts it on the floor, against the concrete wall.

Everybody, they're standing around in their shorts, juggling their wallets and car keys, cell phones, and whatnot.

Me bringing a bouquet of roses, wilting and all, more junk to juggle, it was just plain stupid.

Getting undressed, I was unbuttoning my shirt, and the stopwatch girl giving out paper bags, she points at my chest and says, "You planning to wear that on camera?"

She's holding a bag marked with the number "72." The clothespin clipped to one paper handle. My number. The stopwatch girl points her gun finger at my chest, and she says, "That."

Tucking my chin, I look down until it hurts, but all I can see is my crucifix on the gold chain around my neck.

I ask if that's a problem. A crucifix.

And the girl reaches out with the clothespin, squeezing it open. She jabs to pinch it on my nipple, but I pull back. She says, "We've been doing this a long

6

time." She says, "We know to look out for you Bible thumpers." From her face, she could be a high-schooler, about my age.

The stopwatch girl says how the actress Candy Apples, when she set her record with 721 sex acts, they used the same group of fifty men for the entire production. That was in 1996, and Candy only stopped because the LAPD raided the studio and shut down the production.

She says, "True fact."

When Annabel Chong set her early record, the stopwatch girl says, performing 251 sex acts, even with eighty men showing up for the cattle call, some 66 percent of them couldn't get their dicks hard enough to do their job.

That same year, 1996, Jasmin St. Claire broke Chong's record with three hundred sex acts in a single shoot. Spantaneeus Xtasy broke the record with 551. In the year 2000, the actress Sabrina Johnson took on two thousand men, fucking until she hurt so bad the crew had to pack ice between her legs as she sucked off the remainder of the cast. After her royalty checks started to bounce, Johnson went public with the news that her record was bogus. At most, she'd done five hundred sex acts, and instead of two thousand men, only thirty-nine had answered the casting call.

The stopwatch girl points at the crucifix, saying, "Don't try to save anybody's soul here."

The next guy down the table, he pulls off a black T-shirt, his head and arms and chest the same even suntan brown. A ring shines gold, hanging from one nipple. His chest hair lies flat, every hair cropped down to the same stubble size. Looking at me, he says, "Hey, buddy . . ." He says, "Don't save her soul before they call me for my close-up, okay?" And he winks big enough to wrinkle half his face around one eye. His eyelashes big enough to fan a breeze.

Up close, he's smoothed a layer of pink all over his forehead and cheeks. Three colors of brown powder around his eyes, folded into the little wrinkles there. Clamped under one arm, between his elbow and tanned ribs, the guy holds a wad of white, maybe more clothes.

On the other side of the table, the stopwatch girl turns her head to look both ways. She stuffs a hand into one front pocket of her blue jeans, asking me, "Hey, preacher, you want to buy some insurance?" The girl fishes out a little bottle, big around as a test tube, but shorter. She shakes the bottle to rattle some blue pills inside. "Ten bucks each," she says, and shakes the blue pills next to her face. "Don't you be part of that sixty-six percent."

The guy wearing makeup, the stopwatch girl hands him a bag numbered "137," saying, "You want the teddy bear should go in your bag?"

She nods toward the white bundle under the guy's elbow.

Guy 137 whips the wad of white clothing from under his arm, saying, "Mr. Toto is nothing so pedestrian as a teddy bear . . ." He says, "Mr. Toto is an autograph hound." He kisses it, saying, "You wouldn't believe how old."

The stuffed animal is sewed out of white canvas, a long wiener-dog body with, sticking down, four stubby white canvas legs. Stitched on the top, a dog head with black button eyes and floppy canvas ears. Crabbed all over the white canvas is writing, blue, black, and red pen handwriting. Some loopy letters, some block letters. Some with dates. Numbers. A day, month, and year. Where the guy kissed it, the dog's smeared red with lipstick.

He holds the dog in the crook of one arm, the way they'd hold a baby. With his other hand, the guy points out writing. Signatures. Autographs. Carol Channing, he shows us. Bette Midler. Debbie Reynolds. Carole Baker. Tina Turner.

"Mr. Toto," he says, "is older than I myself would *ever* admit to being."

Still holding the bottle of blue pills, the stopwatch girl says, "You want Miss Wright should autograph your dog?"

Cassie Wright, the guy tells us, is his all-time favorite adult star. Her level of craft soars above her peers.

Guy 137, he says how Cassie Wright spent six months shadowing an endocrinologist, learning his duties, studying his demeanor and body language, before playing a doctor in the groundbreaking adult feature *Emergency Room Back Door Dog Pile.* Cassie Wright spent six months of research, writing to survivors and studying court documents, before she set foot on the set for the adult mega-epic *Titanic Back Door Dog Pile.* In her single line of dialogue, the moment Cassie Wright says, "This boat's not the only lady going down, tonight . . ." her west-country Irish accent is dead-on, depicting exactly how hot the steerage free-for-all sex must've been in the final moments of man's worst sea disaster.

"In *Emergency Room,*" he says, "in the lesbian scene

with the two hot laboratory assistants, it's obvious that Cassie Wright is the only performer who knows the correct way to work a speculum."

The critics, guy 137 says, justifiably raved about her portrayal of Mary Todd Lincoln in the Civil War epic *Ford's Theatre Back Door Dog Pile*. Later re-released as *Private Box*. Later re-released as *Presidential Box*. Guy 137 tells us, in the scene where Cassie Wright gets double-teamed by John Wilkes Booth and Honest Abe Lincoln, thanks to her research, she truly does make American history come alive.

Still cradling his canvas dog, its black button eyes against his gold nipple-ring, the guy says, "How much for your pills?"

"Ten bucks," says the stopwatch girl.

"No," the guy says. He stuffs the dog back under his arm and reaches around to his back pants pocket. Taking out his wallet, he pinches out twenty, forty, a hundred dollars, saying, "I mean, how much for the entire bottle?"

The stopwatch girl says, "Lean over so I can write your number on your arm."

And guy 137 winks at me again, his big eye looking bigger inside all that brown powder, and he says, "You brought roses." He says, "How sweet is that?"

3

Mr. 137

You know those days at the gym when you're bench-pressing six plates or you're one-arming your body weight in preacher curls, and one rep you're pumped and stoked, split-setting cable rows with wide-grip pull-downs, you're knocking out reps and sets fast as you can rack the plates—but then, the next set, you're toast. Wasted. Every curl or press is just more effort. Instead of powering through, you're counting, sweating. Panting.

It's not a sugar crash. Wouldn't you know it? The big shift is because some meathead at the front desk has shut off the music. Maybe you weren't *listening* listening, but when that music stops, working out turns into just plain work.

That's the same doom you feel, that drop in blood pressure, when the music shuts off, three in the morning, closing time at the ManRod or the Eagle, and you're left standing still unfucked, all alone.

11

That's the big letdown you'll notice about filming a movie: No underline music. No mood music. Down the hallway, in that room with Cassie Wright, you're not even getting wah-wah electric-guitar porno jazz. No, only after the editing, after looping any dialogue, then they'll add a music track to improve the continuity.

And wouldn't you know it? Bringing Mr. Toto here was a terrible plan.

But scoring a full bottle of Viagra . . . that just might pull me through.

Across the waiting area, the real-life genuine Branch Bacardi is talking to Mr. 72, that kid holding a bouquet of wilted roses. The two of them could be Before and After pictures of the same actor. Bacardi stands in red satin boxer shorts, talking, while one of his hands rubs his own chest in slow circles. In his other hand, he holds a blue throwaway razor. When his rubbing hand stops, his razor hand moves to the same spot, scraping away invisible stubble, the plastic razor scratching in the short, quick strokes you'd use to hoe weeds in a garden. Branch Bacardi keeps talking, never looking down as his rubbing hand roves to another spot, feeling, then pulling the tanned skin tight as the razor hand shaves the skin from every angle.

Right here: Branch Bacardi, star of *The Da Vinci Load* and *To Drill a Mockingbird, The Postman Always Cums Twice* and the first all-singing, all-dancing adult feature, *Chitty Chitty Gang Bang.*

Even indoors like this, Bacardi, Cord Cuervo, Beamer Bushmills—all the male dinosaurs of the adult industry still wear their sunglasses. They pat and smooth their hair. They're the generation of genuine stage actors; they studied their craft at UCLA or NYU, but needed to pay the rent between legitimate roles. To them, doing porn was a lark. A radical political gesture. Playing the male lead in *The Twilight Bone* or *A Tale of Two Titties* was a joke to put on their résumé. After they were bankable legitimate stars, those early jobs would become fodder for anecdotes they'd tell on late-night talk shows.

Actors like Branch Bacardi or Post Campari, they'd shrug their tanned, shaved shoulders and say, "Hell, even Sly Stallone did porn to pay his bills . . ."

Before becoming a world-famous architect, Rem Koolhaas did porn.

Across the waiting room, a young lady wearing a stopwatch on a black cord looped around her neck, she stops beside Bacardi and writes the number "600" on his arm, the six at the top, a zero below it, the second zero below that, the way triathletes are numbered with a thick black felt-tipped pen. Indelible ink. Even as this talent coordinator writes down the outside of each bicep, writing "600" on one arm then the other, Bacardi keeps talking to the roses kid, his fingers probing his own ab definition for stubble, and the plastic razor hovering, ready.

The men who aren't eating potato chips are scratching away with plastic razors. They squeeze pimples. Or they squeeze tubes of goo into their palms, rub their hands together, and smear their faces, their thighs and necks and feet with a coat of brown. Bronzer. Their palms, stained brown. The skin around their fingernails, dirty dark brown. These actors stand with gym bags at their feet, stooping to hunt for tubes of hair

13

gel, bronzer, plastic razors, folding pocket mirrors. They do push-ups, their tidy whities streaked brown. Walk into the only john you get for six hundred actors, a one-holer with a sink and a mirror, and the parade of buttocks have smeared the white toilet seat with layers and layers of brown. The sink smudged with bronze handprints. The white doorway clutched with a haze of brown finger- and palm prints from porn dinosaurs stumbling, blind behind sunglasses.

It's hard not to picture Cassie Wright on the set, sunk into a bed of white satin, by now clutched and smeared and smudged, darker and darker with every performer. Minstrel porn.

I take a pill.

The talent coordinator stops next to me and she says, "Sure, go blind, but don't come to us for a settlement."

I ask her, What?

"Sildenafil," the young lady says, and taps her felt-tipped pen against my hand holding the bottle of blue pills. "Get it hard, but if you overdose, watch out for nonarteritic anterior ischemic optic neuropathy."

She steps away. And I swallow another blue pill.

Talking to the roses kid, Branch Bacardi says, "They don't shoot the performers in order." Cupping a hand to lift one sagging pectoral muscle, he scrapes the razor across the skin hidden underneath, saying, "Officially, it's because they only got three Gestapo uniforms, a small, a medium, and a large, and they got to call dudes to fit the costumes." Still shaving, he looks up and off, watching a monitor mounted near the ceiling that's showing a porn movie. He says, "When it's your turn, don't expect that uniform to be dry, much less clean . . ."

In every corner of the ceiling, you have monitors hanging down, showing hard-core adult films. One is *The Wizard of Ass*. Another plays the classic *Gropes of Wrath*. All of them Cassie Wright's greatest hits. None of them any newer than twenty years old. The monitor Branch Bacardi's watching, it shows him a generation younger, riding Cassie Wright doggy style in *World Whore One: Deep in the Trenches*. That videotaped Branch Bacardi, his pecs don't sag and flap. His arms aren't red with razor burn and rashy with ingrown hairs. The hands gripping, the fingertips almost meeting around Cassie Wright's little waist, the cuticles aren't outlined with old bronzer.

The live Branch Bacardi, the roving hand and his razor hand stop as he stares at the monitor. With his razor hand, he slips the sunglasses off his face. He's still frozen; only his eyes move, snapping back and forth between the movie and the kid's face. Under his eyes hang crushed, crumpled folds of purple skin. Under his suntan, purple veins climb the sides of his nose. More purple veins climb his calves.

The young Branch Bacardi, who pulls out and blows his money shot all over those pink cunt lips, he looks exactly like the kid with the wilted roses. The kid the talent coordinator has marked number 72.

Number 72, cradling his roses, he stands with his back to the monitor, not seeing. This kid is watching the monitor behind Bacardi, the movie *World Whore Two: Island Hopping*, where Cassie Wright deep-throats the erection of a young Hirohito, intercut with shots of

15

the *Enola Gay* approaching Hiroshima with its deadly cargo.

It was after *World Whore Two* won the Adult Video News award for best boy-girl-girl scene, where Cassie Wright teamed with Rosie the Riveter to suck off Winston Churchill, it's that year she took a long sabbatical from moviemaking. One full year.

After that, she went back to her regular schedule of two projects every month. She did the epic *Moby Dicked*. She racked up another AVN award for best anal scene in *A Midsummer Night's Ream,* which went on to sell a million units in its first year of release. Into her thirties, Cassie abandoned films in order to launch a brand of shampoo named "100 Strokes," a lilac shampoo packaged in a tall bottle that curved too much to one side. Stores hated to stock the tipsy bottles, and no one hit the Web site to place orders until she arranged product placements in two movies. In *Much Adieu About Humping,* the actress Casino Courvoisier slipped the bottle inside herself and demonstrated how the long, curved shape bashed the cervix for perfect deep-vaginal orgasms every time. The actress Gina Galliano did the same trick in *The Twelfth Knight,* and retail outlets couldn't keep 100 Strokes in stock.

But wouldn't you know it, Wal-Mart wasn't happy about being tricked into stocking sex toys in the same aisle as toothpaste and foot powder. There was a backlash. Then a boycott.

After that, Cassie Wright tried to stage a comeback, but the monitors here won't be showing any of those movies. Pony Girl films shot for the Japanese market, where women wear saddles and bridles and perform

16

dressage routines for a man cracking a whip. Or fetish movies like *Snack Attack,* a genre called splosh films, where beautiful women are stripped naked and pelted with birthday cakes, whipped cream, and strawberry mousse, sprayed with honey and chocolate syrup. No, nobody here wants to see her last project, a specialty film called *Lassie Cum, Now!*

Among industry insiders, the rumor is that the movie we're shooting today will eventually be marketed as *World Whore Three: The Whore to End All Whores.*

The moment in *World Whore One* when the doggy scene shifts to three doughboys liberating a convent of French nuns in Alsace, as the new scene starts, Bacardi slips on his sunglasses. Without her habit and wimple, one of the nuns has a thong tan-line. None of the nuns have any pubic hair. Bacardi's fingers stroke the skin around one nipple, and the razor starts to scrape.

The talent coordinator with her stopwatch and black pen walks past me, saying, "Those are hundred-milligram pills, so look out for dizziness . . ." Counting on her fingers, she says, ". . . nausea, ankle and leg swelling . . ."

I take another pill.

Across the room, Branch Bacardi leans forward a little and reaches both hands around to the small of his back. With one hand, he stretches out the elastic waistband of his boxer shorts. With the other, he sticks the plastic razor inside the red satin to start shaving his butt.

The talent coordinator walks away, still counting. ". . . angina," she says, "irregular heartbeats, nasal congestion, headache, and diarrhea . . ."

That year, the one full year that Cassie Wright took

off at the height of her movie career, industry insiders
rumored that she had a child. A baby. She got knocked
up doing a reverse cowgirl, when Benito Mussolini lost
his load inside her. You hear how she put the baby up
for adoption.

Wouldn't you know it? Mussolini was played by
Branch Bacardi.

And I take another pill.

4

Sheila

Sweat collects.

Sweat pools as pale blisters inside my two layers of latex gloves. Borrowed an old precaution from gay porn: you wear a blue condom inside a regular pink condom, that way, if the dick turns blue in the middle of anal sex, you know the outside rubber's busted. A failsafe. True fact. Wearing pink gloves on top of blue gloves, my fingers feel hot, pulsing with my every single heartbeat; sweat collects in bubbles that rove just underneath my latex skin, merging with other blisters of sweat, melting together. Growing. Bulges of sweat swell in fat pads across my palm. Sweat squirts past my knuckles, inside the latex, to balloon my fingertips, swollen and soft. Numb.

I feel nothing. Just my own pulse, and the sweat crawling around inside my skin.

The latex, smudged with brown tanning crap. Orange with potato-chip flavor or dusted white with powdered

19

sugar or cocaine. Smeared red from money stained with barbecue sauce or blood.

Feel the other blisters—could be my hand curls into a fist around a ballpoint pen, or my fingers pinch a dollar bill—and other blisters race backward to the wrist of the gloves, bursting hot and wet down my forearm. The trickle of sweat, cold by the time it drips from my elbows.

Some pud-puller holds a fifty-dollar bill, a hand gripping each end so he can snap it tight. His hands tug the bill tight a couple times, making a pop-pop sound. Another pop-pop sound. Standing so close the dripping head of the pud-puller's dick touches my hip. Soft as a kiss. A tiny battering ram.

A couple more pops, and I look at him. Step back. Look down at the shiny string drooping between my blue-jeans leg and his dick head.

The pud-puller slides his fifty onto my clipboard, saying, "Listen up, baby. I only get an hour for lunch." Saying, "My boss is already gonna kill me . . ."

I shrug my shoulders. Wipe my wet elbows against the sweat stains at the waist of my T-shirt.

All that today comes down to is free will.

Do you allow adult individuals to make their own legal choices?

These pud-pullers. These jerk jockeys. You only need to look at them to read their minds. Take, for example, the kid with the armful of roses. Sees himself as some Prince Charming. Shows up today to rescue Cassie Wright from her tragic lifetime of poor choices. Half her age. Thinks, one kiss and she's going to wake up and weep with gratitude.

Those are the losers you need to keep your eye on.

Gang-bang protocol, ever since Annabel Chong first called the shots, it says all the guys have to wait, shlong-out naked. Ms. Chong, her fear was some crazy with a gun or knife. Some Holy Roller, hearing direct orders from God, would answer the casting call and murder her. True fact. So—all six hundred pud-pullers have to stand around almost bare-assed.

All that today comes down to is free trade.

Do you restrict a person's ability to earn income and exercise personal power?

Do you restrict their behavior in order to prevent them from possibly being hurt? What about race-car drivers? Rodeo bull-riders?

These chicken chokers. Didn't bother to read any feminist theory beyond that outdated Andrea Dworkin tripe. Nothing sex-positive. Nothing along the lines of Naomi Wolf. *I come, therefore I am . . .* No, whether a woman is a concubine to fuck or a damsel to redeem, she's always just some passive object to fulfill a man's purpose.

These monkey-milkers. One waves me over, pointing his index and middle fingers at the ceiling and flicking them toward himself, the way he'd flag a waiter in a restaurant. My eyes lock onto his. I walk over. This loser lifts his other hand, opening the fingers to show me a folded fifty-dollar bill he's got palmed. The money, limp and translucent with popcorn butter. Damp from bottled water. Greasy with red lipstick at one end. The loser slips the fifty onto my clipboard, saying, "Check your list, honey, and I think you'll find I'm next . . ."

Bribe money.

Officially, word is we have a random-number genera-
tor. Whatever number pops up, that's who gets to go
onto the set.

Pull the fluorescent pen from my seat pocket. Draw
a line across the bill to test is it fake. Hold the fifty up
to the light of a monitor to look if the magnetic metal
strip runs through it. In the movie, Ms. Wright's ass
squirms behind the money.

Tucking the fifty under my top sheet of names, I
write down the loser's number. Meat-beater 573. Under
that top sheet, flattened out, you can feel a thick layer
of fifties and twenties. A couple hundreds. A fat mattress of cash.

Ask me, Ms. Chong's best skill was crowd manage-
ment. It was her idea to bring the men onto the set in
groups of five. Among those five, the first man got erect
was the one got to screw her. Each group was on set
for ten minutes, and whoever was able got to ejaculate.
Even if some guys never got hard, never touched her, all
five counted toward the 251-man total.

The real genius was to make it a competition. The
erection race. Plus, studies show that when males are
placed together in close proximity before a sex act, their
sperm count will rise. These studies are based on dairy
farms, where bulls will be staked in groups near a fertile
cow. The resulting harvest will yield greater volumes of
viable semen. Stronger convulsions of the pelvic floor,
maximizing the height and distance of expelled semi-
nal fluid.

The science behind a good money shot.

Increased affinity and surface tension. Higher viscos-
ity. The physics of a good facial.

A biological imperative, only better. Basing porn films on modern dairy-farm procedures. Trade secrets that can destroy the romance of any good gang bang.

True fact.

Want to drag the bottom for every loser, every pervert with issues around intimacy, men completely unable to reveal themselves and terrified of rejection—you want a cross section of those bottom feeders—just run a couple newspaper ads seeking male performers for a gang-bang feature.

According to the British anthropologist Catherine Blackledge, the human fetus begins to masturbate in the womb a month before birth. At thirty-two weeks, that ripple, that twitching within the uterus, isn't the baby kicking. The nasty little thing starts jerking off in the third trimester and never, ever stops.

This crew of pud-pullers, these ham-whammers, it's they who killed the Sony Betamax. Decided VHS over Beta technology. Brought the expensive first generation of the Internet into their homes. Made the whole Web possible. It's their lonesome money, paid for the servers. Their online porn purchases generated the buying technology, all the firewall security that makes eBay and Amazon possible.

These lonely jerk jockeys, voting with their dicks, they decided HD versus Blu-ray for the world's dominant high-definition technology.

"Early adopters," the consumer electronics industry calls them. With their pathological loneliness. Their inability to form an emotional bond.

True fact.

These pud-pullers, these jerk-offs, it's them leading

the rest of us. It's what gets them off that decides what your million kids will want for Christmas next year.

Across the room, another loser catches my eye, his arm raised, flicking the air with a folded fifty pinched between two fingers.

Want to talk third-wave feminism, you could cite Ariel Levy and the idea that women have internalized male oppression. Going to spring break at Fort Lauderdale, getting drunk, and flashing your breasts isn't an act of personal empowerment. It's you, so fashioned and programmed by the construct of patriarchal society that you no longer know what's best for yourself.

A damsel too dumb to even know she's in distress.

You could cite Annabel Chong—real name: Grace Quek—who fucked that first world's record of 251 losers because, for once, she wanted a woman to be "the stud." Because she loved sex and was sick of feminist theory portraying female porn performers as either idiots or victims. In the early 1970s, Linda Lovelace was delivering exactly the same philosophical reasons behind her work in *Deep Throat*.

The last thing today comes down to is personal growth.

Do you respect someone's right to seek challenges and discover their true potential? How is a gang bang any different than risking your life to climb Mount Everest? And do you accept sex as a form of viable emotional therapy?

It only came out later, about Linda Lovelace being held hostage and brutalized. Or how, before becoming a porn star, Grace Quek had been raped in London by four men and a twelve-year-old boy.

Early adopters love Annabel Chong. The damaged love the damaged.

True fact.

Counting the money padding my list of names, my latex fingertips turn black from touching the bills. Another loser steps up, almost close enough his dick touches me. Asks about the T-shirts, where are the T-shirts? Matches my stride as I cross the concrete floor, step by step, staying at my elbow.

I tell him, "Thirty dollars, cash." He'll get the chance to buy a T-shirt as he leaves the building. The souvenir caps, they're another twenty bucks. To reserve an autographed copy of the feature, we're talking $150.

Ms. Wright's already signed the covers, the slip sheets for inside the boxes. Just in case God sends meatbeater 573 the divine order to strangulate her. Or God sends Ms. Wright a stroke. Sends an earthquake or a tidal wave.

Another last thing today comes down to is reality.

What do you do when your entire identity is destroyed in an instant? How do you cope when your whole life story turns out to be wrong?

Sweat balloons inside my gloves—still pink, so both layers of latex are still intact. My fingers pruned, wrinkled, from swimming so long. The skin pickled and old. My defenses still intact. Safe and clean, but feeling nothing, too old for the twenty-year-old rest of me.

Across the room, in the light of a dozen porn movies, another two fingers flicker. Wave hairy knuckles. Hooked for me to come over. Holding more bribe money, folded to hide inside a fist.

25

5

Mr. 600

No shit, I told kid

72 a lie about the uniforms, how they was shooting us out of order since they only rented the three Gestapo getups. The kid's watching the movies we got playing overhead. For the movie, we're talking *On Golden Blonde*. His eyes squirming with twin reflections of Cassie Wright, same as two tiny video monitors, his jaw hung wide open, the kid don't give a rat's ass what I got to say.

I tell the kid, "Don't expect she's going to look that good . . ."

Kid 72's eyes—light brown, same as mine used to look.

The girl up there, sucking the clit of Boodles Absolut, that girl used to say how she was going to rule the industry someday. That sweet young Cassie Wright, the way she told it, she could lick anybody in the world.

But, looking around this room here, the motley collection of dicks they cattle-called today, I'd say how her career's turned out the other way around.

Kid 72 rolls his eyes all over Cassie and Boodles.

"That's a joke I made," I tell him and give him the elbow. Today, anybody in the world can lick her . . .

Some dude across the room, holding some kind of teddy bear under his arm, keeps eyeing me. Dude number 137, with a gold ring through one nipple. We're talking stalker material here.

Really, I tell the kid, he'd better hope he gets called soon. The production company's got a reason they're calling this *The Whore to End All Whores*. Won't nobody be setting a new record after today. What we do here will stand for the rest of human history. This kid, me, dude 137 staring at us—after today, we'll have a place in the record books.

Kid 72, his eyes twitch and shift around on that video screen. His hands hold those roses close in and high against his chest, as if the flowers aren't already garbage.

I tell him, "Don't expect Cassie Wright is going to live through this . . ."

No, it's got nothing to do with only three Nazi uniforms. The wrangler calls back number 45, then number 289, then number 6, some crazy order of guys, but really it's to hide the fact that those cameras will run even after Cassie Wright slips into a coma. There's dudes here who will do the deed thinking she's just asleep. Ain't no human body that can take a pounding from six hundred hard-ons.

We're talking one pussy fart getting pounded in too deep. Or eating snatch, one puff of air up inside her

27

works and a bubble gets into her bloodstream. An embolism. That bubble zigzags all the way to her heart or brain, and it's a fast fade-to-black for Cassie Wright.

Saying this, I'm watching another video monitor, Cassie blowing some dude in *World Whore One*. Dude's lips plumped thick and red as a fag's asshole. Great triceps definition. No fuzz on his nut sack. I take off my sunglasses, and that dude up there is me.

Kid 72 keeps watching *Golden Blonde*. Dude 137 keeps watching us.

The reason they're shooting dudes out of order is so the editor can cut the pop shots together, one to six hundred. After that, Cassie will moan and flop around as much with number 599 as she does with number 1. In between, she'll only lie there like she's sleeping, but really in a coma. Or worse. Nobody here, none of us shmucks, will know any different than the official press release: "Adult Superstar Dies After Setting World Sex Record."

Sure, she's been in training. Kegel weights. Aerobics. Pilates. Yoga, even. Hard, as if she was set to swim the English Channel, but, hell, in the room back there, playing mattress underneath six hundred dudes—she's being the English Channel.

"Another joke," I tell the kid and give him the elbow.

But the truth is, won't nobody call any ambulance until the set's struck and this project is in the can.

No, any inquest happens, and every dick here will swear she was alive when he was humping away. We're talking major denial. After that, the American public will piss and whine. To get media time, religious do-gooders will climb on the bandwagon. Rabid feminist types. The government will step in, and no babe will ever set any new record of 601.

Cassie will be dead, but us six hundred dicks here, we'll go into the history books. Half us dudes will springboard off this—first-timers launching new careers, old-timers making comebacks. Every one of us wearing a T-shirt printed "I'm the Dick That Killed Cassie Wright."

Cassie Wright will be dead, but her backlist of videos, everything from *The Ass Menagerie* to her all-facial compilation *Catch Her in the Eye* to the classic *A Separate Piece*, will turn into solid gold. *Bang the Bum Slowly*. Boxed collector-edition sets. The eternal Marilyn Monroe sacrificial goddess of adult entertainment.

This kid 72 keeps glued to the video monitor.

The wrangler comes by, the Sheila babe, and she scribbles "600" down my arms. Says, "Don't shave off a nipple," and nods at the razor in my hand, the triple blades buffing the shadow from under my pecs.

I ask her, "Who's the vulture?" The dude with the teddy bear. Number 137, eyeballing me.

This babe Sheila flips some pages on her clipboard, dragging a fingernail down the list of names and numbers. "Wow," she goes. "You'd never guess." Sheila points her fingernail at my abs and goes, "You missed a spot."

We're talking my treasure trail; it's not symmetrical.

Still shaving, I ask, "Do I know him?"

Sheila goes, "You ever watch prime-time television?"

Holding the razor, I tap the "600" on my arm, saying how I outrank her, saying she needs to quit being a tease and tell me the dude's name. No need to re-mind her what happens to this project if I bail. If Cassie Wright fucks six hundred dudes, she's a world-beater, and this company has the season's top product. But if Cassie fucks 599 guys, she's just a big slut. And the company ain't got jack shit to market.

And this tease, she winks at me. This wrangler babe, she says, "You're a bright guy. You'll figure it out . . ." And the tease walks off.

Dude 137, he's still looking at me. Holding that bear. Some big-time player with a name and a face, slum-ming from the TV.

Next to me, kid 72 says, "Hey." He's looking at me instead of the video, and he goes, "Weren't you . . ." He cocks his head slantwise, squints up his light-brown eyes, and goes, "Didn't you use to be Branch Bacardi?"

Jerking my head toward dude 137, I ask, "What's his name?"

And kid 72 looks and says, "Wow. That detective from the series on Thursday nights."

The razor's sliding across my abs, looking for pull, for the resistance of little hairs nobody can see yet. I ask the kid, what series?

What's the dude's name?

Why's he staring at me?

But the kid's back to eyeing the video. Kid 72 nods at the screen, going, "You think I look like her? Cassie Wright. You think we look alike?"

His brown eyes still on the scene of Cassie and Boo-dles, not even looking at me, the kid says, "No reason." He goes, "I'm just asking."

Across the room, dude 137 touches one fingertip to a spot on his chest. Touching his gold nipple-ring. He points his index finger at me, then looks down and taps his chest again.

And, looking down, we're talking a long black line of blood just flooding out from my nipple.

6

Mr. 72

A guy eating po-
tato chips at the buffet they laid out, a second guy steps
up next to him. The second guy, across his back is the
number "206," not only felt-penned, but tattooed in
thorny, fat blue letters, the two on one shoulder blade,
the zero on his spine, the six on his other shoulder. The
guy cramming his mouth with potato chips, chewing and swallowing as his hand brings up more from
the buffet table, a steady crunch-crunch loud as somebody walking on gravel, his arm lifting chips has "206"
scribbled down the bicep.

The tattooed guy stoops a smidge, bending his knees,
then stands fast and backhands the first guy across
the face. Putting his whole body into the hit, the tattooed guy's hand, the clap sound, leads a long spray of
spit and potato crumbs toward the ceiling. The smack
echoes, dull with the impact of hard knuckle bones
knocking skull bones with almost nothing in between.

Those knuckles padded by only a glove of hairy skin. The skull only cushioned with a cheekful of chewed potato crud and salt.

With the potato-chip guy coughing on the floor, the tattooed guy twists his shoulders sideways. His slapping hand still raised high in the air, he points his gun finger down at the numbers spread across his back. He says, "Two-oh-six . . . my number." He bends to meet the eyes of the man on the floor and says, "Get other number." Still twisting one arm to point at his own back, he says, "Is *mine*."

A red wash of blood pulsing out his nose, the potato-chip guy keeps chewing. Swallows. He wipes his lips with one hand, smearing red across one cheek. Wipes again, making a blood mustache straight across both cheeks.

The girl carrying the clipboard and wearing a stopwatch on a cord around her neck, she walks over to the two guys and says, "Gentlemen." Taking a handful of paper napkins off the buffet table and giving them to the guy with the bloody nose, the girl says, "Let me settle this."

The nosebleed guy sniffs back the blood and reaches for another handful of potato chips. His lips, swelled up with salt, split open and leaking blood.

As the girl's flipping through the papers on her clipboard, the guy numbered 137 steps up beside me. The guy from television. With the autograph dog. He says, "Someone certainly wasn't breast-fed . . ."

The stopwatch girl is crossing out the number on the potato-chip guy's arm. She's writing a new number.

The tattooed guy lowers his arm, watching them.

Rubbing the knuckles of that hand in the palm of his other hand.

"Him with the tattoo," I say, "the guy's in a Sureno street gang from Seattle." I tell number 137, "He killed somebody, served twelve years in prison. Been out since last year."

Guy 137, hugging his autograph dog to his chest, he says, "You know him?"

I tell the guy, "Look at his hand."

On the web of skin between the thumb and gun finger of one hand, the tattooed guy has two short parallel lines with three dots along one of the lines: the Aztec symbol for the number thirteen—Aztec numerology and Nahuatl language being popular with the Sureno gangs of southern California. On his lower back, just above the waistband of his boxer shorts, is a scrolled fancy tattoo of the number "187": the California Penal Code section for murder. Next to his bellybutton is a tattoo of a tombstone with two dates, twelve years apart, recording the sentence he served.

Guy 137 says, "Are you in a gang?"

My adopted dad taught me.

Other guys around the room, I point out their tattoos. The Asian guy with black stripes tattooed around his bicep, he's a member of the Japanese mafia, the Yakuza, and each black stripe stands for a crime job he's done. Another Asian guy, the "NCA" tattooed across his back brands him as a member of the Ninja Clan Assassin crime family. Standing, walking around, waiting their turn are guys with a little crucifix on the skin between their thumb and gun finger. Three little lines sticking up mark the tattoo as a Pachuco Cross, the sign of Hispanic gangs. Other guys have three dots tattooed to form a triangle on that same spot. If they're Mexican, those three dots mean *Mi vida loca.* "My crazy life." If the guy's Asian, the dots mean *To o can gica.* "I care for nothing."

Guy 137 says, "Your dad was in a street gang?"

My adopted dad was an accountant for a big Fortune 500 corporation. Him, me, and my adopted mom lived in the suburbs in an English Tudor house with a gigantic basement where he fiddled with model trains. The other dads were lawyers and research chemists, but they all ran model trains. Every weekend they could, they'd load into a family van and cruise into the city for research. Snapping pictures of gang members. Gang graffiti. Sex workers walking their tracks. Litter and pollution and homeless heroin addicts. All this, they'd study and bicker about, trying to outdo each other with the most realistic, the grittiest scenes of urban decay they could create in HO train scale in a subdivision basement.

My adopted dad would use a single strand of mink hair to paint the number "312" across the bare back of a tiny street-gang figure. To make a member of the Vice Lords of Chicago. It's how gangsters declare their turf— they get a tattoo of the telephone area code, usually across their upper back. Sometimes their chest or belly. The guy who hit the potato-chip guy, he's laid claim to the Seattle area code—what should be Norteno turf. I say it's no wonder he's so defensive.

Members of the Blood gang always cross out the

"C" in any of their tattoos. To deny any allegiance to the rival Crip gang. If someone has a tattoo with a "B" crossed out, that shows he's a Crip.

"Your dad taught you that?" says guy 137.

My adopted dad. Working on his model-train set. He never cheated on my adopted mom, but he could spend days photographing hookers and painting tiny figures to match them. He'd never take illegal drugs, but his tiny junkies or meth freaks, each one was a little masterpiece. Using a needle-thin paintbrush, my adopted dad would tag the walls of dinky factories and miniature abandoned tenements and flophouse hotels.

I tell guy 137 I'm sorry his TV series got canceled last season.

Number 137 shrugs. He says, "So you're adopted?"

And I tell him, "Only since I was born."

Waiting his turn with Cassie Wright, a flabby blond guy with a long beard stands with both arms folded across his chest. His yellow beard so stiff and coarse the hair juts straight out from his chin, not falling down with gravity. Maybe so dirty. His pale forearms are blotched with blurry black A's and B's, swastikas, and shamrocks. Prison tattoos pricked with a broken guitar string, inked with the soot from burned plastic forks and spoons mixed with shampoo. The Aryan Brotherhood. Tattooed spiderwebs cover both his big, freckled elbows.

Near the Aryan guy, Mr. Bacardi hooks a finger in the gold chain around his own neck. At the lowest point of the chain, dangling over his throat, hangs a gold heart. A locket Cassie Wright's worn in a zillion scenes.

Bacardi pinches the gold locket between his thumb and gun finger and slides it back and forth along the neck chain.

"My real mom," I say, "she's a big star in movies, but I can't say who." I say how I've written tons of letters to her, care of her production company and distributors, even the agent that handles her, but she's never wrote back.

Guy 137 looks down at the flowers I'm holding.

"It's not that I want money or for her to love me," I say. "All I'm after is just to meet her. How I figure it, right now I'm the age that she must've been when she had to give me away."

If her agent or somebody is intercepting my letters and trashing them, I don't know. But I have a secret plan to someday meet her. My real mom.

Number 137 says, "You know your real dad?"

And I shrug.

Across the room, a black guy, the back of his shaved head is tattooed with a flag rippling, the flag bearing the number "415," symbol for the Kumi African Nation, a spin-off of the Black Guerrilla Family. At least according to my adopted dad, who'd recite these details as he held a magnifying glass in one hand and a paintbrush in the other, doctoring the little train figures that came from Germany as doctors, street sweepers, policemen, and hausfraus. Poking them with specks of new paint, he remade them as members of La eMe, the Mexican mafia; the Aryan Warriors; the 18th Street Gangstas. If I stood next to him and put my hand on his basement workbench, if I held still, my adopted dad would paint the "WP" and "666" for White Power at the base of my thumb. Then he'd tell me, "Hurry and go wash your hands."

He'd say, "Don't let your mother see."

My adopted mom.

Right now, up those stairs, the lady behind the door, she's neutral territory. A shrine where you pilgrimage a thousand miles on your knees to pay tribute. Same as Jerusalem or some church. Special to white supremacists and Bloods, Crips, and Ninjas, a lady who transcends turf wars for power. Who transcends race and nationality and family. Every man here might hate every other man, outside of here we might all kill each other, but we all love her.

Our Holy Ground. Cassie Wright, our angel of peace.

Next to me, guy 137 dumps a pill out of the bottle of blue pills he bought. Holding his autograph dog tucked under one arm, he dumps the pill into the palm of one hand and tosses it into his mouth.

Somebody's stepped in the nose blood puddled on the concrete floor. Different sizes of bare feet track bloody, sticky trails in every direction.

I ask what he's doing—right now, I mean—to restart his TV career.

And number 137 says, *"This."* And he shakes the little bottle of pills.

7

Mr. 137

Some humongous
Mexican bitch-slaps this fat slob at the craft-services
table, and then actor number 72, holding the bouquet
of dead flowers, walks over and begins to explain the attack to me. The fight has something to do with model-
train sets and the city of Seattle. The Mexican mafia and
the Vatican. Rattling on, number 72 tells me, "Sorry."

I tell him not to mention it.

"I mean, about your TV series getting canned," he
says.

I tell him to never mind.

"I mean, about all those gossip magazines," he says,
"trashing you."

I tell him to forget it.

And this actor 72 says, "What are you doing, I mean,
here?"

Branch Bacardi, number 600, holds a wad of toilet
paper to his bleeding nipple, and every time I look in

his direction he's looking back at me. Any minute, he's going to walk over here, and I don't have a good opening line ready. The star of *Butt Pirates of the Caribbean* and *Smokey and the Ass Bandit,* and he's cruising me.

Wouldn't you know it?

A person can't simply say, "Hello, Mr. Branch, I absolutely adore your dildo . . ."

Everyone I know, man or woman, keeps your dick in their bedside table. The battery-powered vibrator, or the manually operated regular dildo. Yours is the Goldilocks of dildos: not a long pencil dick, like the one copied from Ron Jeremy's erection. And certainly not one of those so massively big around that you feel plungered like a stopped-up toilet. No, with the length and girth of it, the Branch Bacardi is the one-size-fits-all of celebrity-replica sex toys.

But, no, compliment or not, that kind of dialogue would just never read . . .

Milling all around us, the too-naked men form a sea of tattoos and scars. Rashes and scabs. Stretch marks and sunburns. A catalogue of everything that can go wrong with your skin. Beyond the mosquito bites and pimples, Branch Bacardi stands with Cord Cuervo, the two of their heads leaned together, talking. Bacardi points at me, and Cuervo looks. Cuervo nods his head and whispers into Bacardi's ear, and they both laugh.

I say, let him laugh. The Cord Cuervo Super Deluxe tapers too much; from a circumcised head the size of a pencil eraser, the finger-long shaft spreads to a base big as a beer can. An ergonomic nightmare.

One could always ask Bacardi about the mass-production aspects, the assembly lines in China where

40

sweatshop workers wrap and package endless silicone-rubber copies of his erection, still hot from stainless-steel molds. Or they package and ship jiggling armies of pink plastic vaginas cast from the shaved pussy of Cassie Wright. Chinese slave labor, by hand, tweezing in pubic hairs or airbrushing different shades of red or pink or blue. Accurate down to Cassie's episiotomy scar. Bacardi's every vein and wart. The way people used to make death masks, casting plaster faces of celebrities in the hours between their demise and their decomposition.

Long after Cassie Wright becomes old and demented or dead and rotten, her vagina will still haunt us, tucked under beds, buried in underwear drawers and bathroom cabinets, next to dog-eared skin magazines. Or, showcased in antique stores, Bacardi's rubber erection, priced the same as the hand-carved scrimshaw dildos of lonely, long-dead Nantucket whaling wives.

A kind of immortality.

A person can always ask: How does it feel, that the cock of Branch Bacardi and the vagina of Cassie Wright are reduced to kitsch? Camp *objets* like Duchamp's urinal or Warhol's soup can.

A person could ask: Thanks to the Branch Bacardi Butt Plug, how's it feel to know that people around the globe go to work, to school, to church with your dick wedged up their anus?

How's it feel seeing your dick and balls, or your clit and cunt flaps, cloned a zillion times and sitting on the shelf behind some gum-chewing porn-store clerk? Or, worse, your most private bits heaped in some bargain bin, strangers lifting, squeezing, pinching, and rejecting them the way they would avocados at the super-market?

But, again, this dialogue just does not read.

One could attempt a funny anecdote, a true story about a dear friend. Carl. A huge fan of the Branch Bacardi Super Deluxe. How one morning Carl looked in the toilet and saw thin pink squiggles in his bowel movement. Worms. Ghastly pinworms. But when he carried in a cardboard sample-box of his shit for testing, the lab results came back negative. The pink threads weren't parasites. They were rubber. The pink rubber foreskin of his Super Deluxe had begun to degrade and flake apart. When Carl's proctologist used the word, that's exactly how Carl felt: Flaky. Degrading. Degraded.

One could risk sharing the story about how Carl hooked up with a trick—oh, years ago. And the two men went home together, only to discover they were both big passive bottoms. To satisfy everyone, they shared a two-headed Branch Bacardi special. This happy bumping of sphincters worked fine until—wouldn't you know it—Carl felt his paramour du jour was enjoying more than his allotted half. What had started as a casual, anonymous encounter turned into a savage butt-sex tug-of-war, only with no knot in the rope, no flag to keep one partner from gobbling down all the shared real estate. A greed guard. No Berlin Wall of silicone rubber to keep everyone honest.

Yes, a person might risk such a story, but the last fact a celebrity cocksman like Branch Bacardi wants to hear is that his product is defective.

42

And God forbid Bacardi think I'm Carl. That I've invented a friend to hide behind.

Under my arm, I'm pitted out so badly that sweat's soaked into Mr. Toto's canvas skin, bleaching out Bette Midler's message—"Let's Always Stay Best Friends! Love, Bette"—leaving the words just a blotched blue smudge. Whether it's from the blue pills or feeling nervous, I've sweated out Carol Channing and Barbra Streisand. "Our Weekend in Paris Was Heaven. Yours Always, Barbra."

This actor 72, shifting his bouquet from one arm to the other, he looks at Mr. Toto and says, "What's Goldie Hawn like?"

One can't truly cry, because the Bette Midler was a fake. So was the Carol Channing. And the Jane Fonda. Okay, the truth is, they're all fake. I wrote them all myself, in different handwritings and different colors of ink.

One just cannot approach a star like Cassie Wright with an empty autograph hound. I wanted her to sign her own name among a galaxy of stars. As if we were all close friends.

The truth is, I haven't met any of these women.

After Miss Wright signs, I plan to copy her handwriting and add, "Thanks for the Fuck of a Lifetime!"

One just can't ask a big star like Cassie Wright for that kind of personal inscription. Especially if it's a lie.

And you can't tell an actor like Branch Bacardi that, thanks to his Super Deluxe, you have a callus on your prostate. Even if it's the truth.

His nipple must've scabbed over, because Bacardi's

stopped blotting it with the toilet paper. Instead, he's fingering a necklace. A pendant. Some small gold something hanging from a chain around his neck. Using both hands, he holds the pendant with only his fingertips. Picking with a fingernail, he pops the pendant open and looks inside. It's a locket or a box. No doubt, hidden inside is a little portrait or a lock of hair.

Another form of immortality.

The next time he looks over, if Mr. 600 does approach, perhaps I could tell him about the Vatican, how, if you ask politely, the curators will pull out drawer after drawer to show you the relics within. According to Carl, nested inside some drawers are carved marble dicks. Penises. In alabaster, onyx, obsidian. Row after row, drawer after drawer of ancient pricks, each one numbered, keyed to some masterpiece left castrated. This collection of hundreds of numbered dicks, they were all chiseled off Greek and Roman statues, Egyptian and Byzantine, and replaced with pasted-on plaster fig leaves.

Bronze Minoan pricks, hacked off, small as bullets. Etruscan terra-cotta pricks, crumbling to dust. These priceless wieners, they're nothing the righteous want you to see, but they're still too important to discard.

The same as, inside all those nightstands and glove compartments, all those Branch Bacardi dildos and Cassie Wright vaginas.

I could tell Bacardi that the electric vibrator was first marketed in the 1890s. The first household appliances to be electrified were the sewing machine, the fan, and the vibrator. Americans enjoyed electric vibrators ten years before electric vacuum cleaners and irons. Twenty

44

years before electric frying pans were brought to the market.

To hell with housework, our top priority has always been between our legs.

The talent wrangler walks past me, carrying a potato-chip bag stuffed full of bloody paper napkins from the actor with the split lip. Red blood and orange barbecue flavoring smeared into the white paper. At Branch Bacardi, the young lady stops a moment and he drops his toilet paper spotted with nipple blood into her bag.

Watching the young lady, the boy with his flowers, actor 72, says, "I hate her," his grip crackling, crushing, crumpling the clear plastic funnel holding his roses. His fists squeeze, tighter and tighter, until the thorns poke through.

Watching the talent wrangler, actor 72 says, "How much you want to bet that bitch trashes every letter anybody sends to Cassie Wright, no matter how important what's inside or how much a guy really just wants to tell Cassie how much she means to him?"

If he comes over, that's what I'll tell Bacardi about: those Vatican curators with their dusty drawers full of priceless, faceless, numbered dicks.

Inside his necklace is something no one else can see, but Branch Bacardi looks at it for a long time. Measured by the movies playing overhead, he looks at his secret for a three-way . . . two blow jobs . . . and one clitoral orgasm.

Wouldn't you know it, then Bacardi looks up, at me. And he snaps his locket shut.

8

Sheila

During my initial
pitch meeting with Ms. Wright, I asked her what she
could tell me about a Roman empress named Messalina.

Our pitch meeting, our first face-to-face, we met in
a coffee bar, drinking cappuccinos and bumping knees
under a dinky marble-topped table. Ms. Wright sat
twisted to look out the window. Legs crossed at the
knee, the way that's supposed to give you veins. Eyes
not following anyone walking past. Not watching the
dogs on leashes or the babies in strollers. Not looking
at me, Ms. Wright asked had I ever heard of an actress
named Norma Talmadge?

Or Vilma Bánky? John Gilbert? Karl Dane or Emil
Jannings?

Her false eyelashes made bigger with mascara, not
blinking, Ms. Wright said Norma Talmadge had been
a star in silent movies. The number-one box-office draw

46

in 1923. Got three thousand fan letters every week. In 1927, it was this Norma person who by accident stepped into a patch of wet cement in front of Grauman's Chinese Theatre and started all the movie stars' leaving their hand- and footprints.

A couple of years after the concrete, Hollywood started shooting sound movies. Despite a year working with a voice coach, Norma Talmadge opened her yap and out comes a shrill Brooklyn squeal. Hollywood's top male star, John Gilbert, piped his lines high-pitched as a canary. Mary Pickford, who played girls and young women, barked deep as a truck driver. Vilma Bánky's dialogue was lost in her Hungarian accent. Emil Jannings', in his German accent. Karl Dane's were drowned in his thick Danish accent.

Low clouds kept it dark outside. The awning over the window didn't help. Ms. Wright sat, focused on her own reflection, her eyes and lips reflected on the inside of the coffee-shop window, and said, "John Gilbert, he never made another picture. Boozed himself to death by age thirty-seven. Karl Dane shot himself."

All of these stars, the most powerful actors in film, they were all gone in an instant.

True fact.

What sound movies did to their careers, Ms. Wright said, High Definition was doing the same to a new generation of actors. Delivering too much information. An overdose of truth. Stage makeup didn't look like skin, not anymore. Lipstick looked like red grease. Foundation, like a coat of stucco. Razor burn and ingrown hairs might as well be leprosy.

Like the he-man movie stars who turn out to be

queer . . . or the silent-film actors whose voices sound terrible recorded—the audience only wants a limited amount of honesty.

True fact.

In the past year, Ms. Wright had only been offered one script. A low-budget musical, a fetish vehicle based on the Judy Garland–Vincent Minnelli classic about a sweet, innocent young woman who goes to the World's Fair and falls in love with a handsome young sadist. Called *Beat Me in St. Louis*.

She learned the songs and everything. Took dance lessons. Never got a second callback.

Looking out the window, her eyes fall shut long enough for her to sing, her voice almost a whisper, almost a lullaby. Her face tilts up a tad, as if to catch a spotlight, and Ms. Wright sings, ". . . I got bang, bang, banged on the trolley . . ."

Her eyes peel open, and her voice trails away. Ms. Wright swallows nothing. Slumps to one side, to reach a hand into her purse on the floor. Takes out a pair of black sunglasses. Pries them open and slides them onto her face.

Still looking at nothing outside the coffee-shop windows, not the street full of cars driving by or the sidewalk where people walked. An endless stream of extras. No-name characters opening umbrellas or holding open newspapers to protect their hair. Not watching any of this, Ms. Wright says, "So what's your brainstorm?"

My pitch. How come I've been phoning her agent. Phoned every production company where she's done any work over the past five years. Written letters. Why I'd insisted I wasn't a stalker. Some pud-puller.

I asked, Did she know Adolf Hitler invented the blow-up sex doll?

And Ms. Wright's black sunglasses turned to look at me.

During the First World War, I told her, Hitler had been a runner, delivering messages between the German trenches, and he was disgusted by seeing his fellow soldiers visit French brothels. To keep the Aryan bloodlines pure, and prevent the spread of venereal disease, he commissioned an inflatable doll that Nazi troops could take into battle. Hitler himself designed the dolls to have blond hair and large breasts. The Allied firebombing of Dresden destroyed the factory before the dolls could go into wide distribution.

True fact.

Ms. Wright, her plucked eyebrows arch to show above her dark sunglasses. The black lenses reflect me. Reflect the paper rim of her coffee cup, smeared red with lipstick. Her lips say, "Do you know I'm a mom?"

Her sunglasses reflect me wearing a tweed suit, my fingers slipping the latch, opening my briefcase, leaning forward, my hair pulled back, twisted into a French knot.

For my pitch, I planned to develop a project based on that first sex doll. Work the Nazi angle. Work the history angle. Hammer together a story with genuine educational value.

Ms. Wright's lips say, "Yeah, I had my baby about the age you're at now."

Do this Hitler sex-doll project, do it the right way, I say how it will make a pile of money for that baby. Whoever that baby grew into, Ms. Wright can give

49

him a college trust fund, the down payment on a house, seed money for a business. Wherever that baby has ended up, he'll just be forced to love her.

Ms. Wright turns her face to look at herself, reflected in the window. The reflections of her reflections of her reflections, between the window and her black sunglasses, all those Cassie Wrights shrinking smaller and smaller, until they disappear into infinity.

The religious school she went to, growing up, Ms. Wright said how all the girls had to wear a scarf tied to cover their ears at all times. Based on the biblical idea that the Virgin Mary became pregnant when the Holy Spirit whispered in her ear. The idea that ears were vaginas. That, hearing just one wrong idea, you lost your innocence. One detail too many and you'd be ruined. Overdosed on information.

True fact.

The wrong idea could take root and grow inside you.

Ms. Wright, her sunglasses showed me. Reflected me opening a folder. Taking out a contract. Pulling the cap off a pen and reaching it across the table. My face, flat and smooth with confidence. My own eyes, unblinking. My tweed suit.

Her lips said, "Is that 100 Strokes shampoo that I smell?" She smiled and said, "Now, who was that . . . ?"

The Roman Empress Messalina.

"Messalina," Ms. Wright repeated, and she took the pen.

9

Mr. 600

Kid 72 is easy enough to find, now that his bunch of roses start coming apart, dropping a trail of wilted flower petals to follow him around the room. Dude 72, the kid, his white rose petals follow him as he dogs Sheila around, asking her, "Can I go *soon*?" Looking at the flowers in his hands, he goes, "Is it true?" He goes, "You think she's going to die?"

Dude 137, the television dude, goes, "Yes, young lady, when might we view the body?"

Kid 72 goes, "You ain't funny."

And the Sheila babe says, "Why would Ms. Wright want to die?"

Six hundred of us waiting in one room, we're breathing the same air for the third or fourth time. Almost no oxygen left, just the sweet stink of hairspray. Stetson cologne. Old Spice. Polo. The sour smoke of marijuana from little one-hitter pipes. Dudes stand at the buffet,

51

scarfing down the candy smell of powdered doughnuts, chili-cheese nachos, peanut butter. Dudes swallowing and farting at the same time. Belching up gas bubbles of black coffee from their guts. Breathing out through wads of Juicy Fruit gum. Chewed mouthfuls of pink bubble gum or buttered popcorn. The chemical stink of Sheila's fat black felt pen. The what's-left smell of the kid's rose bunch.

The locker-room smell of some dude's bare feet, we breathe that smell like those cheeses from France that smell like your sneakers in high school that you'd wear in gym class all year without washing them.

Cuervo's laid on his bronzer so thick that his arms stick down the sides of his lats. His feet stick to the concrete floor. When Cuervo takes a step, his skin peels off the floor with the sound of somebody yanking off a bandage.

Our one bathroom we got for six hundred dudes to share, the floor's so wet with piss that dudes stand in the doorway and do their best to hit the sink or the toilet. The reek floating out of that doorway smells bad as any step you ever took when your foot slipped instead of landing, outdoors, slick enough you guess it's a mess before you catch a whiff of the dog turd you'll be digging out the tread of your shoe.

Cuervo lifts one arm, making that bandage sound as the skin peels apart, pasted down with bronzer. Cuervo lifts one elbow and ducks his head to sniff that armpit, going, "Should've brought along more Stetson."

Coming off kid 72, we got the green smell of deodorant soap. The mint tang of mouthwash.

To bait him, I ask dude 137, will this be his first time in front of a camera?

Dude 137 shakes his head, throwing off the smell of cigarettes, under that the smell of his stuffed teddy bear soaked in armpit sweat.

I tell him to go easy on the wood pills. Just now, watching him from across the room, dudes are taking bets on how fast he keels over from a stroke. Dude should see how red his face looks, the veins on his forehead standing out plain as lightning bolts. Either that, I say, or he should get in the pool, put some money down on a time. At least that way he'll make a few bucks when he overdoses.

Kid 72 goes, "Why'd a star like Cassie Wright ever want to kill herself?"

Maybe for the same reason superstar Megan Leigh shot more than fifty-four films in three years and then bought her mom a half-million-dollar mansion. Only then did the star of *Ali Boobie and the 40 D's* and *Robofox* shoot herself in the head.

Isn't a kid alive who doesn't dream about rewarding her folks, or punishing them.

It's how come legendary woodsman Cal Jammer stood in the rain in his ex-wife's driveway and shot himself in the mouth.

It's why pussy queen Shauna Grant died at the business end of her own .22-caliber rifle. And why one night, Shannon Wilsey, the blonde high goddess of porn known as "Savannah," went out to her garage and put a bullet into her head. My money's on the idea that Cassie Wright's set out to cushion the future for some baby she had a long ways back. If Cassie kicks it today, after setting this record, the residuals from *World Whore Three* and her cross-marketed T-shirts, her lingerie and toys, not to mention her backlist of movie titles, that income stream will make her long-lost kid . . . filthy rich. So rich he can forgive old Cassie. For how she got knocked up. How she gave up the baby. That, and the entire fucked-up, screwed-up, sad, wasted way old Cassie lived and died.

If she does the penance of six hundred dudes, Cassie Wright will be forgiven.

Me, personally, I tell dude 137 how I'm adding an embossed slogan to my dildos. Cast in high-relief going around the base, it's going to say, "The Dick That Killed Cassie Wright . . ." On the thickest part, so if you twist it the letters of the writing stimulate the clit.

"You have a dildo?" dude 137 says. On his breath, the smell of flask hooch. The wax-candle smell of lipstick. Dude's wearing tinted lip gloss.

Damn straight, I tell him. A dildo in six different colors, one butt plug, and a double-headed whopper. Plus, I got a life-sized blow-up doll in development.

Dude 137 goes, "You must feel very proud."

Used to be, I tell him, I'd move ten thousand units in a month. My cut on that was 10 percent of the list price. Other dudes, Cuervo for one, they add a few inches to their product. Could be Cuervo starts with a real casting, but what eventually hits the shelf is longer and thicker than he ever dreamed of getting it. Cuervo calls it "artistic license," but it's false advertising. No point calling a product true-to-life if it's not.

Kid 72 stands there, white petals dropping off his flowers. One hand, his fingers are rubbing the little silver cross hanging from the chain around his neck.

Every breath, I feel the gold locket Cassie gave me bumping and pinched between my pecs. Inside that little gold heart rattles the pill. The gold, sticky with blood from my nipple.

"Is that really Cord Cuervo?" says dude 137. Squinting to look through the fog of dope smoke and cologne, dude 137 goes, "The star of *Lay Misty for Me* and *The Importance of Balling Ernest?*"

Nodding my head. And *Lady Windermere's Fanny,* I tell him. All classy, high-brow projects. I wave at Cord, and he waves back.

Number 49. Number 567. Number 278. The dudes that Sheila calls back, they each pick up their sack of clothes and follow her up some stairs. Nobody but Sheila comes out. My bet is, once you're done, they exit you out some other way. No risking that some dude will backtrack and tell us what to expect. The legal standard for a gang bang is called "instances of sex," meaning any hole—her cunt, ass, or mouth—and any instrument—your dick, finger, or tongue—but for only one minute. No, you follow Sheila through that door, and a minute later you're gone. Whether or not you cum, you'll find yourself undressed and shoved out some fire exit, pulling on your pants in the alley.

Dude 137, still squinting across at Cord, says, "Now, that's a pathetic sight." He nods at Beamer Bushmills and Bark Bailey, going, "Imagine the person who could stay in that pubescent mind-set and devote his life to lifting weights and ejaculating on cue. To remain so

55

aggressively retarded, arrested in such early-adolescent values, until he wakes up as a saggy, flabby, middle-aged train wreck."

Swear, the dude looks square at me when he says the "train wreck" part, but maybe he was just looking at me. I say there's worse that can happen. A dude could end up cast a couple seasons in a prime-time hit TV series, then lose the role because of some messy sex scandal, then find he's so associated with the old series—maybe playing some dopey private detective—that he'll never get another decent acting job the rest of his career. I say that would be genuine tragic.

And I tell dude 137, in case he wants to cover his bald spot, I got a spray in my bag that might work. Pointing with my toe—I always wear flip-flops on a shoot—with my big toe I show him the trail of hair that follows him. Rose petals or bronzer or hair, we all leave our tracks.

Looking from his hair on the concrete, then to me, then to Sheila checking her clipboard across the room, dude 137 yells, "Chop-chop." He yells, "You want to goose it a little, honey?"

I ask him, does he got some better place to be? Some audition, maybe? Not me, I tell him. I can wait. I say, because of what we do today, to that woman back there, some kid she's never met will never have to work another day in his life. The way today works is, I have to be Mr. Last.

Looking at kid 72, the dude goes, "One has to wonder how many children have been sired by those men, making the films they do." Looking at me, dude 137 goes, "If indeed we all leave our tracks."

It's never happened, I say.

And dude 137 goes, "Nice locket." He reaches a hand toward Cassie's necklace, the little gold heart pasted with blood between my pecs, his fingernails shining, buffed bright and clear-coated.

10

Mr. 72

I tell those guys, "Porn babies." Shaking my roses at the 137 guy and Branch Bacardi, I say, "They exist." Petals fluttering everywhere, I say, "There are kids who get conceived during adult movies. I mean, when those movies get made."

Mr. Bacardi shakes his head, saying, "Urban legend."

Guy 137 says, "Love child."

"That's a stretch," Mr. Bacardi says, "to call anything conceived during an all-leather backdoor dog-pile gang-bang video a 'love child.'"

And I tell them that's not funny.

The 137 guy says, "No, wait." He says, "Rumor is, there was a kid conceived during *The Blow Jobs of Madison County*."

Mr. Bacardi says, "No." Shaking his head, he says, "She terminated."

And guy 137 says, "That's what the industry calls an 'outtake.' "

I tell them that's really not funny. My hands shake so hard the petals pile up around my feet.

And Branch Bacardi asks me, "Who, then? Can you name even one performer who had a porn baby?"

I point up at a video monitor, where Cassie Wright's wearing rice powder on her cheeks and ink-black geisha eye makeup, playing a lovely demure Japanese-American heroine in *Snow Falling on Peters.* Cassie Wright, I tell them. She had a child.

Her folks live in Montana, I say, where her mom still works for the local school district and her dad does dry cleaning. Twenty years ago, they say, Cassie came home and told them she was pregnant. Cassie didn't look pregnant. She'd bleached her hair and dieted away half herself. She was driving a Camaro so new it still had dealer plates, painted midnight black. Their little girl told them she'd just shot her first masterpiece, *World Whore One,* and she tried to explain to them about an internal pop shot. The way, sometimes, it doesn't work perfectly. Cassie said she'd been late for three weeks and pissed hot on a pregnancy stick. She'd asked to stay with them until she'd had the baby, and they'd told her no. *World Whore* had made Cassie an instant star, and her hometown was too small for people not to recognize their prodigal daughter.

In secret, her mom mailed her money every week. So did her dad. To an address here in the city. But they never saw the baby.

Guy 137 and Branch Bacardi just look at me. Guy 137 holding and petting his stuffed dog. Mr. Bacardi fiddling with the gold locket around his neck, rolling it between his thumb and gun finger.

"Parents," Mr. Bacardi says, "they'll screw you up every time."

This isn't a joke, I say. Porn babies, they're more than just the by-products of the sex industry. The leftover veal calves of adult entertainment. A spin-off product like new strains of hepatitis and herpes.

Guy 137 lifts his hand, wiggling the fingers in the air, until I stop talking.

"Hold on," he says. "I have to ask: what's an internal pop shot?"

I stare at him a beat.

Mr. Bacardi says, "I can take that one."

I nod my head for him to take over.

Branch Bacardi looks up and clears his throat. His voice flat and even, as if he were reading from a book, he says, "The male performer achieves orgasm inside the female performer, without wearing a condom. After he withdraws, the female performer contracts her pelvic floor with enough force to forcefully expel the ejaculate from her vaginal orifice."

Any color drains down from the 137 guy's face. Pale and wide-eyed, he says, "Hardly the best form of birth control . . ."

My point exactly.

But, Mr. Bacardi says, you can't wear condoms and expect your product to sell in Europe. His head still tilted back, he's looking at *Snow Falling on Peters,* where Cassie Wright is being marched at bayonet point and shipped off to a Japanese-American internment camp.

Still fingering the locket, Mr. Bacardi says, "She was so pretty . . ."

Guy 137 sighs, saying, "The face that caught a thousand facials."

My point is, these kids aren't a joke. Or an urban legend.

Another sprinkle of rose petals spiral to the floor.

Branch Bacardi says, "But can you name one?"

On the monitors, Cassie's embroidered silk kimono slides to the dusty floor of her barracks in the Nevada desert. In the background bubbles a hot tub overflowing with giggling women, their faces powdered white with rice flour. Pouring sake on each other's bare breasts. The internment-camp commandant walks into the barracks, carrying a coiled whip.

My roses are almost nothing left but stems and thorns.

The girl with the clipboard and stopwatch is walked all the way across the room, over next to the food. With my free hand, I wave for Mr. Bacardi and guy 137 to lean in closer. Keeping my voice lower than the noise of the whip cracking, I whisper.

Tapping the tip of my gun finger to my chest I mouth the word "Me."

I'm not a joke or a legend.

I am that porn baby.

11

Mr. 137

Wouldn't you know

it? It's the damned shampoo. That "100 Strokes" crap
Cassie Wright launched. So what if the bottle's the
perfect shape for . . . But wash, rinse, and repeat for a
couple days, and you'll go bald. All this damage just so
maybe Miss Wright will smell it in my hair and con-
sider it a compliment.

Not that she could smell anything. The place reeks
like a stockyard.

Shaking his head, Branch Bacardi looks through the
shifting herd of naked men. Pointing at actor 72, where
he stands in a pool of white rose petals across the room,
Bacardi says, "Dude there?" Bacardi says, "Little dude's
a total boner-kill." The finger he's pointing, he turns
that hand, cupped palm up, and Branch says, "Dude,
spare me some wood?" Cupping his brown hand, the
palm stained the same bronzer as the fingers, Bacardi
shoves his hand at me. His brown eyes look at me. They

look at his open hand. Look at me. Bacardi says, "A pill, dude?"

I tell him to take his own.

Shaking his head, Bacardi says, "Didn't bring none."

Shaking my head, I say I need my stash. The pill inside his pretty little heart-shaped girly-girl locket, I tell him. Bacardi should swallow that.

Touching the gold locket, where it rests between his shaved pecs, Branch lets his mouth crack open. His Adam's apple jumps with a swallow. Tapping the locket, Branch says, "Ain't that kind of pill." He says, "Dude."

Standing across the room, as far as he could walk without leaving the building, actor 72 stands, one hand rubbing the little silver cross that hangs from his neck chain. Rubbing the cross between his thumb and index finger. His green eyes looking everywhere but at Bacardi and me. The actor's other arm still cradles the bouquet of roses.

"Besides," Bacardi says, tapping the locket so hard his chest echoes with a deep, hollow thump, "this here's for a friend." He says, "I'm just safekeeping it."

He's Branch Bacardi, I tell him. He won't need some crutch to perform.

"You're Dan Banyan, dude," Bacardi says.

Was Dan Banyan, I tell him.

Actor 72, he drops his top-secret maternity bomb, then hangdogs it away from us, fast, his bare feet slapping the concrete floor. Stomping hard as anybody can against cold concrete, sprinkling rose petals every step.

"Banyan dude don't need pills," Bacardi says, his bronzer arm bent to keep that hand out, the bicep and triceps jumping inside his skin. Flexing and relaxing, his number "600" expanding and shrinking, his arm has a life of its own. Breathing. "Dude like Dan Banyan, private-detective dude, wasn't you, like, banging ten walk-ons every episode? Every babe client and witness and, like, lawyer," Bacardi says. "Dude's a babe meat grinder . . ."

Nodding after number 72, I say, "You have to admit, he does look like her."

Above the young man, the television hanging over his head shows Miss Wright's groundbreaking civil-rights statement about racism, the sexy comedy where a fresh-faced college sophomore comes home for Christmas and tells her doting parents that she's dating a chapter of the Black Panthers. It's called *Guess Who's Coming at Dinner*. Later re-released as *Black Cock Down*.

"Dude," Bacardi says, "I'll pay you, after." His hand out, he says, "Promise."

I put another pill between my lips, leaving one fewer in the bottle.

"Fifty bucks," Bacardi says. "Cash."

And I swallow. Nodding at number 72, I tell Bacardi, "That troubled young man looks a great deal like you also."

Bacardi looks. At the actor with his roses. Then at Miss Wright stretching her lips around a fat black erection. And he says, "Didn't happen."

Looking at the locket on his chest, the gold shining pink through a dried layer of his nipple blood, I say, "Just take your own pill."

"That's how come I'm in the business so long, dude," Bacardi says. "My whole life, I never shot nothing but blanks." Snapping his fingers at me, Bacardi says, "One pill and I'll sign your teddy bear you got."

Mr. Toto. The pen's still hooked behind one dog ear. I shrug, Sure. And I hand him over to Bacardi. The brown fingers take the canvas dog, and I wait.

Bacardi's eyes fixed on his writing, scratching the pen down the dog's canvas leg, Bacardi says, "You met Ivana Trump?" He looks up at me. "And Tina Louise? Like in *Gilligan's Island*?" He says, "What's she like?"

His teeth, those kind of too-white caps. The white of subway tiles and police cars. Public-bathroom white. The man by whom all other men have measured themselves for a generation. The biggest woodsman in porn.

I ask, Are you really sterile?

Bacardi holds Mr. Toto, turning the dog and looking from name to name. "Lizbeth Taylor," he reads. "Deborah Harry . . . Natalie Wood . . ." He hands the dog back, saying, "I'm impressed." Mr. Toto's canvas is smudged with bronzer, brown fingerprints. Bacardi's signature is a huge "B," a second huge "B," both letters trailing off into illegible black-ink scrawls.

I take Mr. Toto from him, telling him, "And now the fifty dollars."

Bacardi snorts, his shoulders slumping, rounded, and his mouth hanging so slack that his heavy, square chin hides the locket, almost resting on his shaved pecs. "Dude . . . ," Bacardi says, "how come?"

Now, me with my hand out, cupped palm up, I say, "Because Dan Banyan was a lot of house payments and car payments and credit-card interest ago. Because right now you need a pill and I need the funds."

From across the room, number 72's walking this way. Not all at once. He takes a couple steps to the buffet, where he eats a potato chip. He takes another step to stand next to the talent wrangler, says something in her ear, and she flips through the sheets on her clipboard. All this time, he's working a big circle back toward Bacardi and me.

The talent wrangler shouts, "Gentlemen, may I have your attention?" Looking at her clipboard, she shouts, "May I have the following three performers . . ."

Men at the buffet stop chewing. The veterans freeze, the plastic razors hovering over the leather of their calf muscles and glutes. The men holding mobile phones to one ear, or wearing cordless headsets, they stop talking, silent, and lift their heads to listen.

"Number 21 . . . ," the wrangler shouts. "Number 283 . . . and number 544." She smooths the papers on her clipboard and lifts one arm straight overhead to wave her hand in the air. "Right this way, gentlemen," she says.

I shake the pill bottle, half empty now, so the remainder of the pills rattle, and I say, "That was a close call." I say, "Now, fifty dollars, or take that pill you're safeguarding."

Branch Bacardi breathes in, the pecs and lats and obliques of him ballooning huge, and he breathes out one long, breath-minted sigh. "So," he says, "you really hung out with Dolly Parton?"

My pulse pounding in my ears, I close one eye. Open it. Close my other eye. Open it. I'm not going blind, not yet.

And a voice says, "Can I talk to you?" A man's voice.

66

Wouldn't you know it? Here's number 72, standing close by, only a couple steps behind Bacardi and me.

One of his brown fingers tapping the gold locket, the fingernail outlined in darker brown, Bacardi says, "This pill, one of them miracle drugs." Tapping the locket, he says, "Don't matter what's wrong, dude, this here will cure you." His smile flat-lines, those fake teeth disappeared behind his tanned lips, and Branch Bacardi says, "This baby will cure anything."

To the young man, number 72, I lean over a little, brushing my fingers over the top of my head so he can see, and I say, "Is my hair really getting thin?"

12

Sheila

Ms. Wright jogs along a sidewalk, her knees pumping waist-high in front of her, thighs stretched tight inside black bicycle shorts. Breasts bouncing, swinging side to side, strapped inside a white sports bra. Elbows bent L-shaped, hands limp and flapping loose at each wrist. Feet slapping the concrete sidewalk in tennis shoes.

Her stomach skin, tight and tan. No stretch marks. Nothing to show for being a mother.

At her crotch, the black spandex stretches to cover a small bulge. Bigger than camel toe. Swelling bigger than moose knuckle. Way bigger than a clit. Ms. Wright's crotch swells, bulges, bounces. Another stride, her foot stamping concrete, and the bump inside her bicycle shorts starts to inch down one spandex leg.

We're jogging alongside a park of green grass. Ms. Wright, glancing at the pages of a three-ring binder

I carry. Each page, a clear plastic sleeve that shows six Polaroid snapshots. Each picture a man's head and shoulders numbered in black felt-tipped pen along the bottom edge. The six hundred–plus vein-drainers who signed aboard our project. These shank-shuckers and baby-barfers. The tadpole-tossers who passed their hepatitis screening. With one hand, I grip the top edge of the binder, pressing it into my waist. My other hand turns each page, my fingers twisted around a pen.

With every footfall, the binder bruises my bellybutton. The heavy hundred-plus pages.

The bump inside Ms. Wright's shorts, it stops a moment, hung up by the elastic band around the bottom of the leg. The spandex and elastic bend, blossom, burp, and a pink ball drops, shining wet, bouncing one, two, three dark spots of damp on the gray concrete.

Ms. Wright says, "Fuck." Whispers the word, slapping her leg where the ball slipped out.

The pink ball bounces four, five, six spots backward on the sidewalk behind us. Seven, eight, nine wet spots, and a dog leaps from the grass to snatch the ball in its teeth. This black dog—sleek as a seal on stick legs, small as a cat with pointed ears—its black gums snap shut on the pink ball, and the dog races away across the grassy park.

Stopped, watching the dog shrink, smaller and farther, Ms. Wright says, "You know that movie, *Wizard of Oz*?" She says, "The dog that played Toto was a cairn terrier named Terry." Watching her pink ball disappear in the distance, Ms. Wright says, "In the scene where the witch's guards, they chase Toto out of the castle, in the final take, one of the guards, halfway across the castle drawbridge, he made a flying tackle and landed on poor Terry. Broke the Toto dog's back leg."

The dog was off the picture for weeks. True fact.

Back to jogging, her knees pumping, her hands flapping loose, Ms. Wright keeps talking. That same *Wizard of Oz* movie, the actor Buddy Ebsen almost died from an allergic reaction to aluminum dust, part of his costume as the Tin Woodsman. The actor Margaret Hamilton was supposed to leave Munchkinland in a ball of flames, only the flash fire ignited her green copper-oxide makeup, setting fire to her face and right hand.

Buddy Ebsen lost his part to Jack Haley. Margaret Hamilton lay in bed for six weeks, wrapped in gauze and Butesin Picrate.

Ms. Wright glances down at the six Polaroids I'm holding. The next six cum-casters and pudding-pullers. Jogging along, she says, "Actors have done lots worse stuff for their craft."

The pink ball, she says it was molded from silicone. Two-point-five ounces. Twenty millimeters in diameter. A Kegel exercise. You put the ball inside and tense your pelvic floor. Used to be, Asian women would insert two metal balls with mercury inside their hollow cores. The mercury would shift all day, rolling the balls, stimulating the women, getting them hotter as the weight of the balls strengthened their pussy muscle. Their husbands came home, and those revved-up housewives would fuck them at the front door.

True fact.

Too bad the mercury would tend to leak out, Ms. Wright says. Drive them nuts. Poison them to death.

Nowadays, most Asian girls go around with jade balls inside. The stronger you get, the more weight you can carry.

Jogging now, the crotch of her shorts swell. The spandex stretches thin, the color going from black to dark gray. Another stride, and something pops out the elastic leg. Thuds on the sidewalk, ricocheting, skipping, skidding, to land in the gutter. Round as a tennis ball, white, but smooth and veined as marble or onyx stone.

It's a Kegel-exercise stone, Ms. Wright says, stooping to lift it with both hands. Two and one-half pounds. Wiping the stone against the leg of her shorts, brushing dead leaves and grains of dirt from it, Ms. Wright says, "A couple months of hauling this, and my pussy could go to the Olympics . . ."

All of this, training for *World Whore Three.*

She says a real movie star is willing to suffer. In that *Singin' in the Rain* movie from 1952, the actor Gene Kelly danced the title song, take after take, for days, with a fever of 103 degrees. To make the rain look right on film, the production used water mixed with milk, and there was Gene Kelly, dog-sick but splashing and soaked in sour milk, smiling happy as the best day in his life.

In 1973, some movie called *The Three Musketeers,* Oliver Reed got to sword-fighting in a windmill, and somebody stabbed his throat. Just about bled him to death.

Dick York trashed his spine while filming a movie called *They Came to Cordura* in 1959. Kept acting despite the pain until 1969, as the witch's husband in *Bewitched*. Spent fourteen episodes in the hospital and lost the role.

Ms. Wright shrugs her shoulders, still jogging, her hands tossing the exercise stone back and forth, the weight making her biceps muscles pulse big with each catch. She nods for me to turn the page. Trading this crop of ceiling-spacklers for the next six weasel-teasers.

Turning the plastic page, I tell how Annabel Chong compared a gang bang to running a marathon. Sometimes you felt full of energy. Other times you felt exhausted. Then you'd get your second wind and feel your energy rise.

The actor Lorne Greene, Ms. Wright says, who did the TV show *Bonanza,* years later he was filming his other show, *Lorne Greene's New Wilderness,* and an alligator bit off his nipple.

Saying this, she's looking at the Polaroids. Her knees pumping, her boobs bouncing, her eyes stay fixed on one single picture. A young carpet-seeder. Number 72. Same eyes as her, same mouth. Nice. Not somebody who'd bite off your nipple.

For my part, I've tried to pace the gang bang the way Messalina would, spreading out the ugly yogurt-yankers, the old and obese bone-honers, the dirty and deformed gland-handlers as far as possible. A monster inserted between every eight or ten ordinary sea-monkey sprayers.

Ms. Wright nods at a familiar face, joystick-jerker

number 137, and she says, "He's hot . . ." A washed-up TV ham looking to toss some baby gravy.

At Ms. Wright's crotch, something new swells under the black spandex. The bump jiggles down her leg. Pops under the elastic. Flashes bright green across the sidewalk and is gone into a storm drain, rattling, banging, pinballing down metal pipes in the dark.

"Fuck," Ms. Wright says, watching it gone, "that one was genuine jade."

The two of us, heads bent to stare into the iron grate of the storm drain, I say how Aristotle used to write philosophy while holding a heavy iron ball in one hand. The moment he'd start to fall asleep, his fingers would relax, and the ball would crash to the floor. The noise woke him, and he'd keep working.

"Aristotle?" Ms. Wright says. She looks from the storm drain to me.

Yeah, I say. True fact.

Ms. Wright's eyes squint, narrow, and she says, "The man who married Jackie O?"

And I say yeah. Turn the clear plastic page in my three-ring binder. Show her another six Florida-floggers.

Ms. Wright tells me how the famous lover Casanova used to stuff two silver balls inside the ladies he was dating. He claimed it prevented pregnancy, the silver did, because it was a tiny bit poison. The same reason why folks wanted to eat food with silverware, because silver kills bacteria.

Vaginal weights, she calls them. Some ring with bells inside them. Some could be little rolling pins. Some in the shape of chicken eggs. You carry them while you run or bicycle or do housework.

73

Jogging along, tossing the stone from palm to palm, where it lands with a hard clap, Ms. Wright says, "My only beef with jogging is when I rattle." She says, "Sometimes I feel like I'm a can of spray paint."

The stone smacking into her other palm, the sound of one hand clapping.

I turn another page in my three-ring binder. Another six fly-fishers.

At rifle rubber number 600, Ms. Wright says, "Good ol' Branch Bacardi . . ." Looking into the distance, the green grass horizon where the dog disappeared, Ms. Wright says, "That cairn terrier? That little dog Terry, who played Toto in the *Wizard of Oz* movie? You know that pooch is still around?"

When the dog died, the owners had Terry stuffed and mounted. In 1996, the dog sold at auction for eight thousand dollars.

True fact.

"Toto wasn't even a boy dog. Terry was a girl," Ms. Wright says. "Even dead, that girl is still making people money."

Something round and heavy, it's already inching down one leg of her shorts.

13

Mr. 600

The Sheila babe yells for everybody to shut up. She checks the call sheets and says, "Number 21 . . . I need number 21."

We're all not breathing, fingers crossed, ears pointed to hear our number.

Checking her clipboard, Sheila goes, "Number 283 and number 544." One hand, she waves for dudes to follow her onto the set, saying, "Right this way, gentlemen."

On the monitors, we're looking at Cassie Wright wearing a white slip, playing a frustrated Southern belle desperate to fit into her husband dude's rich plantation family. The dude's a used-to-be semi-pro pitcher who drinks too much and ain't slipped her the bone for so long she's worried he's queer. Cassie's fretting about her dad-in-law, named Big Daddy, and her nieces and nephews she calls little no-neck monsters. Rubbing her hands up and down her white satin hips, Cassie says, "I feel . . ." She says, "I feel like a twat on a hot tin roof."

This here was later released as *Slut on a Hot Tin Roof.*

Later re-released as *Cunt on a Hot Tin Roof.*

Cord is playing the maybe-queer husband, and, sitting in a wheelchair, he goes, "Well, jump on, Maggie! Jump on!"

Only nobody's watching. We're all eyes squinted, watching Sheila and the three dudes, waiting for them to get to the top of the stairs, when Sheila swipes her mag card and the door to the sound stage clicks open. All of us dudes, holding one hand with the fingers spread to block that blast of bright light, the spots and fill lights, halogen bulbs, and the glare off Mylar reflectors, so bright it hurts to look. But dudes look, anyway. The side of every face flashed white as the dark shapes of Sheila, and the three dudes melt and disappear into the bright white.

Dudes still waiting, squinting, mole-eyed blind, and peeking through eyelashes, we can't see nothing but maybe white skin against white sheets, white-blond hair and fingernails, all that faded under white, white, baking-bright lights. The smell of bleach, ammonia, some cleaner. And a draft of cold air-conditioning.

In that flash, the silver cross the kid wears, the gold locket I got from Cassie, they both spark and flare, hot with caught light for just one heartbeat.

Dudes' eyes start to adjust, and the door's already closing, closing, closed. Our basement we're waiting in, the floor gummy with spilled soda and potato-chip crumbs sticking to dudes' bare feet, this here's that much darker after just that look. Our peek at bright nothing leaving us blind.

76

I'm touching the necklace Cassie gived me, the locket, saying something to the television dude with the teddy bear.

And kid 72 shows up at my elbow, asking to talk.

"Not to you," the kid says to the 137 dude. Kid's fingering something that hangs from a chain around his neck, the little silver cross, a church kind of cross, and the kid goes, "I need to ask Mr. Bacardi something."

My bet is the television dude, number 137, has got some dirty blood running inside him. He shrugs and goes off, but not too far, just a couple steps.

To the kid I go, this is me poking my finger in the kid's face, I'm going, "Dude, you here to help your old lady or punish her?"

The kid's, like, all shaking his lips, no, going, "I'm here to save her."

The reason babes in this business, why they don't do some birth control, is because the pill can make your skin break out. Give you greasy, stringy hair. The diaphragm or the sponge is nothing you want in your works, not if you're double-teamed with a pair of professional dicks like Cord or Beam or yours truly. No babe doing a double penetration wants anything wire tucked up inside her, I tell the kid. It ain't half impossible he's the son of Cassie Wright.

"She put me up for adoption," he goes. "She tried to give me a better life. I only want to return the favor."

I go, "By busting in there?"

"If that's what it takes," the kid goes, sticking his chin at me.

By busting in and embarrassing Cassie when she's focused on setting her world's record that's going to revive her career? Embarrass her in front of the crew and all her professional colleagues? I go, "Kid, don't be doing her that kind of favor."

Standing around, the four, five hundred dudes shift from one foot to the other. Dudes stare at the monitors hanging from the ceiling, Cassie Wright riding cowgirl on the boner of Cord Cuervo as he sits in his wheelchair, she's bracing her weight with one arm planted on the plaster cast of his fake broken leg. The fact nobody's walked out, it's a testimony to what dudes will endure for a piece of ass. If there was a free, hot piece of snatch waiting on top of Mount Everest or on the moon, we'd have a high-speed elevator already built. Commuter space flights every ten minutes.

"Kid," I go, "believe it or not . . ." I'm tipping my head toward the stairs, the locked door, the lights and set behind it, and I go, "The lady up there, she don't want to be saved."

And the kid goes, "I knew you wouldn't under-stand."

His flowers he's holding, the leaves and petals went twisted and dark.

The kid goes how, when he was little, he come across the picture of a lady on the Internet, more than pretty, and he couldn't not surf to look at her every day after school. In the picture, she was naked and playing some wrestling game with some naked superhero muscle guys. The private parts of them were showing, but they were all trying to hide them inside each other. Some tag kind of game. The kid sounded out the letters of her name listed under the bottom of the picture, and they said "Cassie Wright." He typed those letters into the Internet, and a lot more naked pictures popped up.

Pictures and video clips, a million zillion results the kid had to track down.

"Dude," I go, "the legal standard is 'instances of sex.' " I go how the kid can tell her his feelings. Say, "Thank you, Mommy." Tell Cassie he loves her. But it's not impossible he maybe slips a finger inside? Maybe, reaching to hug her, his little finger by accident sticks in her ass? I go, "Dude, that way it's a win-win."

The kid only shakes his head, going how he grew up with her pictures, hunting her movies, learning everything about her. When his balls dropped, his obsession only got worse.

"Dude," I go, "stop being so selfish. This is her big day."

One afternoon, the kid goes how he was beating off and forgot to lock his bedroom door. His adopted mom must've got home from work early, and she walked in on him and started hollering. She caught him.

"Dude," I go, "in flagrante?"

"No," kid 72 goes, "beating off."

The kid's adopted mom starts yelling, asking if he knows who that woman is. Does this kid know who he's fantasizing about? Does he have any idea, any inkling about the identity of that slut? The kid's there with his dingus in one hand, a Cassie Wright split-beaver shot on his monitor, and his adopted mom just goes on and on.

"Dude," I go.

"She's yelling," the kid goes. "She's screaming: 'That's your birth mother.' "

His adopted mom's yelling how he's pounding pud to pictures of what's probably his own conception.

"Dude," I go, "if Cassie don't get fucked by six hundred dudes today, she's screwed."

And the kid 72 goes, "I can't." He's fingering the silver cross, going, "Maybe if I talked to her first, maybe then I could." He goes, "But ever since my adopted mom said what she said, since she told me the truth, I haven't been able to . . ."

The kid looks down at his limp, wilted flowers.

And I snap my fingers, holding my arm straight up in the air—I'm snapping my fingers, throwing my voice at the television dude. I'm going, "Teddy-bear dude, we got an emergency here." I go, "The kid needs a pill or nobody's getting famous today."

A light flares, high up and way off to one side. The door at the top of the steps swings open, and a black shape stands outlined. "Gentlemen," the shape says, "I need the following numbers . . ."

And, my hand in the air, I'm still snapping my fingers, waving to get help our way.

14

Mr. 72

How I told it to Mr.

Bacardi, that wasn't the whole deal. Not even half the
story. When I first downloaded clips of Cassie Wright,
I wanted to see her maybe knitting a regular ordinary
thing, I don't know, out of yarn. Or I wanted to watch
her cooking a pan of something on a stove. Just, I guess,
reading a book in a chair next to a lamp in a nice room
without gallons of hot jizz all over her.

On bulletin boards, online message boards, where
fans post details about every mole and eyelash Cassie
Wright has, every color lipstick she's wore, guys dissect
every blow job, I don't know, like it was for college-
homework extra credit. Cassie Wright was born in
Missoula, Montana. Her parents are Alvin and Lenni
Wright. They live in Great Falls these days. And, yes,
Cassie Wright had a baby she gave up nineteen years
ago.

Surfing the Web, I looked for pictures of her vacuuming carpet. Driving a car. With her clothes on and nothing getting stuffed inside of her.

Some money orders I mailed, and nothing ever came back. But the first package I got was a Cassie Wright pocket vagina, the premium, limited-edition, numbered version. Number four thousand two hundred. Totally museum-quality. Mint condition. Small enough I'd carry it to school in my jeans pocket, with my left hand tracing the folds and soft hairs of her. In Modern American Studies, I'd sit in the back row with my left fingers Brailling, blind, deep in my pocket, until I knew every fold and wrinkle by heart. Ask me the state capitals of Wyoming or Phoenix, and I'd shrug. But ask me anything about the pussy flaps of Cassie Wright, and I could draw you a map.

That pocket vagina, you could press the clitoris and it would pop out. Press it back inside the hood. Press again to make it pop out. I could do this until my fingertips were red raw, about to bleed. I slept with it under my pillow.

My teacher Mr. Harlan, in my Dynamics of Science class—one day, handing back papers, he saw the calluses on my fingertips, already cracked and dark pink, and he asked if I was learning guitar. I don't know. Let's just say those hours and weeks of constant pleasure weren't doing Cassie Wright's vagina any good, either.

Let's just hope, looking at some of the six hundred guys here today, that the real deal is more durable than the latex version. As the vagina started to break apart, I saved newspaper-delivery money until I could send away for a previously owned Cassie Wright latex breast replica. I could only afford the left one, but anybody

82

would tell you it's the better of the two. Of course, it's too big to fit in my pocket, too big for under my pillow. It's too big to do anything but collect dust under the bed.

So I mowed lawns. I returned pop bottles for the deposit. I walked dogs. Washed cars. Raked leaves.

This part I didn't tell Mr. Bacardi. How could I?

Winters, I shoveled snow. Cleaned the black, stinking crud out of roof gutters with my bare hands. Washed St. Bernards. I hung Christmas lights and trimmed hedges.

Nighttime, I'd squeeze my breast replica. Rub the dusty nipple against my lips. Lick it. Tweak it between two fingers until I fell asleep.

I drained and changed the oil in big four-door automatic-trannie old-lady cars. Needing the money to buy a Cassie Wright replica, fully realistic sex surrogate, that makes you pretty much the bitch slave of every old lady in town. I don't know.

I went trick-or-treating for UNICEF, and those worm-eaten, starving kids in Bangladesh didn't see one nickel of the thirty bucks that folks donated.

The day the brown package arrived in the mail, my adopted mom called me at school to ask should she open it.

Let's just say I panicked. I told the worst lie a kid can. Told her, No. I said it was a gift—her special, secret Christmas present that I'd sent for to surprise her.

On the phone, I could hear my adopted mom shaking the box. She said, "It's so heavy." She said, "I hope you didn't spend a fortune."

Shame, shame on me.

Those lawns I mowed, the dogs walked, the cars washed, I told my adopted mom all that work went into buying her the best dream present ever, because she was such a great, wonderful, loving, terrific mother.

And on the phone, her voice melted, saying, "Oh, Darin, you shouldn't have . . ."

When I got home, the package sat on my bed. Heavier than you'd guess, a weight between a big library dictionary and a St. Bernard. My adopted mom was gone to her cake-decorating workshop, and my adopted dad was at work. With nobody else in the house, I peeled open the box, and inside, all folded and wadded, looked like some pink mummy. Leathery and wrinkled as a peat bog mummy from the *National Geographic* magazine.

The online auction sold it as being brand-new, a virgin, but the blond wig smelled like beer, and the hair felt patchy where it was pulled out. The inside of each thigh felt sticky. The breasts, greasy. On the bottom of one foot, I found the sort of stem you'd see on a beach ball. So you could blow her up.

I unrolled her across my bed and started to blow.

I blew, and her breasts rose, they fell, they rose. I blew, and some wrinkles went smooth, but then came back. I blew air into the bottom of her foot until lightning spots flashed in my eyes.

Right now, here and now, while I'm waiting to hear my gang-bang number called, the girl with the stopwatch walks past, and I put out my hand. To make her stop, I touch her on the elbow, just my fingers on the inside of one elbow, and I ask if it's true. What Mr. Bacardi's telling guys. Could Cassie Wright die today?

"Vaginal embolism," the girl says. She looks at me, then her eyes go back to the sheets of names on her clipboard. Still running her pen down the list of names, she marks a check next to one guy. The girl twists one hand and looks at the watch on her wrist. She checkmarks next to another name. She says it takes a puff of air equivalent to blowing up a balloon, but due to the dense blood supply in a woman's pelvic region, you can force a bubble of air into her circulatory system. "If a woman is pregnant," the girl says, "it's even easier."

In one case from 2002, she says, a woman in Virginia was using a carrot for stimulation and died from an embolism, but anything with an odd shape might trap and force pockets of air into the bloodstream. Other documented cases include batteries, candles, pumpkins.

"Not to mention," the girl says, "soap on a rope."

Vaginally or rectally, it can happen in either hole.

"Every year," she says, "an average of more than nine hundred women die this way."

Each woman dies within seconds.

"If you need facts and figures," she says, "then I recommend *The Ultimate Guide to Cunnilingus* by Violet Blue. Or the article 'Venous Air Embolism: Clinical and Experimental Considerations' from the August 1992 issue of *Critical Care Medicine*."

The girl looks at her watch again and says, "Now, if you'll excuse me . . ."

I don't know . . . pumpkins?

All those years ago, blowing air into my Cassie Wright surrogate, I almost blacked out before I heard the hissing. A faint, soft whisper of air escaping.

After filling the bathtub with water, dragging the

85

pink skin of her down the hallway, I held her under to look for bubbles from a leak, my hands spread under water, holding her submerged while her blond hair swam around her face and her eyes stared up. Dead. Drowned.

Bubbles swelled at the sides of her neck. Bubbles outlined her nipples and the flaps of her pussy. Wide half circles of little holes, leaking air. Teeth marks. Bites through her pink skin.

My adopted dad's train set, he uses every plastic and glue you can find. With her pink skin spread over the mountains and villages of his plastic landscape, I daubed rubber and epoxy, doctored with clear nail polish and acetate, until I'd healed every bite mark.

From my adopted mom's dresser, the bottom of the underwear drawer, I borrowed a lacy honeymoon nightgown that had been buried there forever in layers of tissue paper. I borrowed the pearl necklace that my adopted mom never wore except to church on Christmas. Dressing the surrogate, I said every opening line from every Cassie Wright video I'd seen. Brushing the blond wig, I said, "Hey, lady, did you order a pizza?"

Wiping my adopted mom's lipstick on the lips, I said, "Hey, lady, you look like you could use a nice back rub . . ."

Spraying on perfume, I said, "Relax, lady, I'm only here to check your pipes . . ."

On my computer was playing a pirate copy of *World Whore One,* and whatever Lloyd George did, I did the same. Pulled down the pink thong panties. Unhooked the push-up bra. Lloyd and I were both laying pipe when Cassie's breasts went from a D cup to a C. By

86

now my dick was bumping mattress. She was leaking, losing air. The faster I pumped, the flatter she went. From a C cup to an A. Shriveling and wrinkling underneath me, wasting away. The more I pumped, the more Cassie Wright's face collapsed, caved in. Her skin felt loose, baggy, and slack. With my every push, she aged a decade, dying, dead, and decomposing as I hurried, faster, pounding mattress, rubbing myself raw in my rush to get off. Pumping this pink ghost. This murdered outline down the middle of my twin bed.

Each woman dies within seconds.

I never heard the door open behind me. Didn't feel the draft of air on my bare, sweating ass. I didn't turn around until I heard the voice of my adopted mom. Her honeymoon nightgown. Her Christmas pearls. On my computer, Lloyd George blowing his load down the side of Cassie Wright's beautiful face.

My adopted mom, behind me she yells, "Do you have any idea who that is?"

And I turn, my bone stuck straight out, a pole still wrapped in pink latex, me waving a flag shaped like Cassie Wright.

And my adopted mom screams, "That's your birth mother."

That, the last boner I would ever sprout.

No, I never did tell Mr. Bacardi that part.

15

Mr. 137

First opportunity, I sidle up and ask the talent wrangler how it is she knows so much about vaginal embolisms. Almost a thousand women dead every year? Killed by carrots and batteries forcing air inside them? That seems like a remarkably rarefied set of facts for anyone to reference offhand.

"Sorry," I tell her, "I couldn't help overhearing."

Holding one end of a ballpoint pen, the wrangler taps it like a wand in the direction of each man still here. Her lips silent, making the shape of each number— 27 . . . 28 . . . 29—she writes something on her clipboard, at the same time saying, "That's why Ms. Wright pays me the big bucks."

The wrangler is Cassie Wright's personal assistant, project researcher, gofer, she says. Looking at her wristwatch, scribbling some numbers, an equation, on the top sheet of paper, the wrangler tells me, "She asked me to assess the risk."

I ask if it's true. Does Miss Wright have a grown child?

"It's true," the wrangler says and looks up at me. White flakes cling to the shoulders of her black turtleneck sweater. Dandruff. Her straight black hair, she's tied it back in a ponytail, not a hair hanging loose. The trailing hairs frizzed and bushy with split ends.

I nod my head, just tilt my neck a little toward the kid, number 72, and I ask, "Is it him?"

And the wrangler looks. Her eyes blink. Look. She shrugs, saying, "He certainly does look as if he could be . . ."

Every week, Cassie Wright gets a pile of letters from a different thousand young men, each of them convinced he's the baby she gave up for adoption. As part of her job, the wrangler has to open this mail, sort it, sometimes respond to the letters. An easy 90 percent of them are from these would-be sons. All of them begging for a chance to meet. Just one hour of face-to-face so each kid can tell her how much he loves her. How she's always been his one true mother. The one love he'll never be able to replace.

"But Ms. Wright's not an idiot," the wrangler says.

Cassie Wright knows, the moment you make yourself available to any man, he starts to take you for granted. Maybe the first time she meets her son he'll love her. But the second time, he'll ask her for money. The third time, he'll ask for a job, a car, a fix. He'll blame her for everything he's done wrong in his life. He'll trash her, rub her face in every mistake she's ever made. Call her a whore if she doesn't hand over what he wants.

"No," the wrangler says, "Ms. Wright knows this isn't about love . . ."

The young men who write, asking to meet. The month after, they write again, begging. Then threatening. They claim to only want to find out their genetic history, any predilection for inherited disease. Diabetes. Alzheimer's. Some claim that they only want to thank her in person for giving them a better life, or they want to show off their accomplishments so she sees that she did the right thing.

"Ms. Wright has never answered a single one of those letters," the wrangler says.

That's why Cassie Wright's largest audience, the only part of her audience still growing, is composed of sixteen-to-twenty-five-year-old men. These men buy her backlist movies, her plastic breast relics and pocket vaginas, but not for any erotic purpose. They collect the blow-up sex surrogates and signature lingerie as some form of religious relics. Souvenirs of the real mother, the perfect mother they never had. Frankenstein parts or religious totems of the mother they'll spend the rest of their lives trying to find—who'll praise them enough, support them enough, love them enough.

The wrangler says, "Ms. Wright knows, even if she found the kid, she'd never be able to meet all those demands."

She looks at Mr. Toto, at the writing on his white canvas skin, and asks, "How'd you meet Celine Dion?"

Overhead, the monitors are showing excerpts from *The Italian Hand Job,* where a team of international jewel thieves are plotting to steal a billion in diamonds from a museum in Rome. During the heist, Cassie Wright distracts the guards by engaging them in a double-penetration three-way. The moment the museum alarms sound, the loud sirens and flashing lights, she clenches her pelvic floor and her jaw, effectively becoming a flesh-and-blood set of Chinese handcuffs and trapping the guards inside herself.

The wrangler holds her ballpoint pen, tapping the air as she counts men around the room. "That's why Ms. Wright's shooting this project," she says.

Guilt.

Guilt and payback.

Especially if Cassie Wright dies, she knows this movie will be the last of its kind. Sales will last forever. Even if it's outlawed here, copies will sell through the Internet. Enough copies to make Miss Wright's sole heir rich. Her one kid.

The wrangler says, "That's not to mention the life-insurance money."

Here's another aspect of the project that she researched: Insurers don't list deaths caused by traumatic gang-bang orgies as exclusions in most life-insurance policies. Not until now. Until six of the top insurance companies will have to fork over payouts totaling ten million dollars upon the death by embolism of Cassie Ellen Wright, payable to her only child. No, Miss Wright didn't want to meet her kid. To her, that relationship was just as important, just as ideal and impossible as it would be to the child. She'd expect that young man to be perfect, smart, and talented, everything to compensate for all the mistakes that she'd made. The whole wasted, unhappy mess of her life.

She'd expect that young man to love her in amounts she knew were impossible.

Across the waiting area, actor 72 stands holding

his roses. His head tipped back, his brown eyes watch Cassie Wright stash several cool millions in diamond ice deep inside her shaved pussy.

"No," the wrangler says. "Ms. Wright wanted to leave her child a fortune, but she wanted the courts to sort it all out with DNA testing . . ."

The wrangler holds up her clipboard so that it blocks one side of my face, one eye, and she says, "Can you see out of this eye?"

I say yes.

She moves the clipboard to block my other eye, unblocking the first, and she says, "How about this eye?"

And I nod yes. I can see out of both.

"Good," the wrangler says. The first sign of Viagra overdose is losing sight in one eye. Half blind, you lose depth perception. She looks around the waiting area, at the crowd of men jerking the half-hard erections still tucked in their shorts, and she says, "Maybe that's why most of you wrote down ten inches on your applications . . ."

I ask, "What about the father? Won't he get part of Miss Wright's fortune?"

The wrangler shakes her head. "Ms. Wright's family," she says, "they disowned her years ago."

No, I meant the father of her child.

"Him?" the wrangler says, staring at me, her mouth hung open, wagging her head from side to side. "The sick fuck who talked her into this awful business? The living piece of shit who slipped her Demerol and Drambuie, then set up cameras and fucked her from every angle?" Rolling her eyes, the wrangler says, "Did you know? He mailed an anonymous copy of that first film to her parents."

That's why, when she went home pregnant, they threw her out.

That's why, to survive, she had to slink back to the sick fuck and make more porn.

The wrangler barks out a laugh. She says, "Why would she leave any money to him?"

No, I say. What I meant was "Who?"

Who was that man, the father of the mystery kid who's about to become rich?

"The sick fuck?" the wrangler says.

I nod.

And wouldn't you know it, she lifts a hand to point her ballpoint pen straight across the room—at Branch Bacardi.

16

Sheila

Valeria Messalina, a descendant of Caesar Augustus, was born twenty years after the birth of Christ and raised in the court of the Emperor Caligula, who—as a practical joke—forced her to marry her second cousin, Claudius, a dimwit thirty years her senior. At their marriage, Messalina was eighteen, her groom forty-eight. Three years later, Caligula was assassinated, and Claudius ascended to the throne.

Once she became empress, according to the historian Tacitus, Messalina fucked gladiators, dancers, soldiers—and anyone who refused her, she had them executed for treason. Slaves or senators, married or single, if Messalina said you were hot—you had to put out.

Talk about giving somebody performance anxiety.

To cleanse her palate between studs and hunks and beauties, Messalina was famous for seeking out the ugliest man in the empire. Fucking him as a sort-of sexual sorbet.

At the time, the most famous prostitute in Rome was named Scylla, and Messalina challenged her to a competition to see who could couple with the greatest number of men in one night. Tacitus records that Scylla stopped after her twenty-fifth partner, but Messalina kept going and won by a wide margin.

The historian Juvenal records that Messalina would go slumming, sneaking into brothels, where she worked under the name Lycisca, gilding her royal nipples with gold dust and selling access to the aristocratic vagina that had birthed her son, Britannicus, the next likely emperor. There she'd work until well after her fellow whores had quit for the night.

At the age of twenty-eight, Messalina hooked up with Gaius Silius and conspired to murder her husband; however, her plot was revealed to Claudius, and he ordered her execution. Messalina refused to kill herself, even as her mother begged her to commit suicide, the only honorable way to end her life. Roman soldiers forced their way into her palace, found her waiting in her garden, and killed her on the spot.

All of this I told to Ms. Wright as we sat in my apartment eating popcorn and watched Annabel Chong fuck her way through 251 jizz-juicers. Groups of five. Ten minutes per group. Sock-soakers. Bone-beaters. The set decorations, the white fluted columns and splashing fountains, a historical re-creation of Messalina's challenge to Scylla. The fake marble and Roman statues. *The World's Biggest Gangbang.* A student in gender studies at the University of Southern California, with a grade point average of 3.7, this film was Chong's tribute to Valeria Messalina.

True fact.

The top-selling porn video of all time: a feminist history lesson lost on countless willy-wankers.

Watching, I asked: How is this any different from the Olympics?

I asked: Why shouldn't a woman use her body any way she wants?

I asked: Why are we still fighting this same battle two thousand years later?

Both of us eating popcorn. No butter. No salt. Drinking diet sodas. Our casting notice already running in a couple newspapers, a news item on a few Web sites. Pud-pullers and palm pilots already calling to get on the list.

Our faces caked in avocado, pore-reducing, collagen-enriched masks. Hair combed with Vaseline and tur-banned in towels. The bowl of popcorn between us on my sofa. The two of us belted in terry-cloth bathrobes. Ms. Wright says, "A take-charge gal like that Messalina was—she shouldn't have let them kill her."

Only a few years after ordering her execution, the Emperor Claudius stuck a feather down his own throat. In A.D. 54, he was pigging out at a banquet, trying to puke so he could eat more, and Claudius choked to death on that feather.

Hearing that, watching Annabel Chong get fucked, it was Ms. Wright who mentioned life insurance. Made me promise to look into a policy. Made me cross my heart, in case anything went wrong, I'd find her lost kid and hand over the insurance payout, plus whatever royalties from the video.

She was still talking how she wanted to make her kid

96

rich when I reached between the cushions of my sofa. Feeling between the popcorn kernels, the old maids, and pocket change until I touched slick paper.

Right there, I handed Ms. Wright the paperwork for six policies. All they needed was her autograph. Total potential payout—ten million.

Without her bifocals, Ms. Wright squints at the paperwork, her avocado mask crumbling, cracking, and flaking green crumbs. She holds the papers at arm's length. Eyeing the fine print, she says. "Always one step ahead, aren't you."

That's why she pays me the big bucks, I tell her. My fingers plucking a ballpoint pen from between the sofa cushions.

And Ms. Wright says. "That empress gal?" Autographing each life insurance policy. Nodding at the television, she says, "That Messalina, she should have just killed herself . . ."

17

Mr. 600

Player dude's yak-king on his cell phone when he goes ballistic. Player dude with his black hair combed, stretched back, and gelled to cover his bald spot, to show a forever space of tall, white forehead, he's yakking stock options and sell prices and reserve margins when Sheila looks up from her clipboard she's holding.

Sheila shepherds the crew of us and yells, "Gentlemen." She yells, "Listen for your number, please. I need . . ."

Every ear turned to listen, tilted up to hear, dudes stop chewing their mouthful of taco chips. Dudes step out the bathroom doorway, their dick still in one hand. Eyes open, wide, looking for the words. Dudes hiss for silence, hold up hands, and pat the air to make other dudes quiet down.

Sheila drops each word heavy as a money shot right in your eye, saying, ". . . number 247 . . . number

354 . . . and number 72." She waves a hand toward the stairs and says, "Would those gentlemen please follow me . . ."

Dude 72, Cassie's maybe kid.

That's when the cell-phone player dude goes ballistic. Dude flats his phone against his chest. Dude's sporting a model shave, where you snap the number-one guard on your clippers and buzz all your chest hair down to the same quarter-inch long. Same as the International Male dudes in the catalogue, but minus the cut muscle. Dude tells his phone, "Hold on a sec." He throws his head back and yells, "This is horseshit, lady!" Yelling after Sheila, dude says, "You think we'll wait all day to drop a wad in some old bag?"

Climbed halfway up the stairs, Sheila stops. She looks back, one hand shading her eyes to see across the hairy ocean of dudes' heads.

Above us on the TVs, the head of Scottish Yard or Interpol or some wop police dude's eating out Cassie Wright in the back of a paddy wagon. His tongue comes across a diamond. Then he's pulling the long string of a diamond necklace out her snatch. Diamonds being her best friend, Cassie is juicing up a storm.

Kid 72, dude with the roses, springs up next to my elbow, saying, "What do I do?"

Fuck her, I tell him.

Kid says, "No," shaking his head. He says, "Not my mom."

Player dude, his arms and legs sport a San Diego tan. Not the rich caramel color of a Mazatlán tan, or the smooth dry brown of a Vegas tan. On his face and neck, that's not the even wipe of a box-bought tan, or

99

deep and buttery, like dudes get in Cancún or Hawaii. Dude's standing there in a cheap, beach-fried San Diego tan, and he's got the nerve to yell, "I'm number 14, and I have places to be. I should've been out of here hours ago."

The number "14" inked on his beige-brown San Diego arm, the player dude says, "This bullshit is worse than the DMV . . ."

Every dude still playing statue, froze, waiting to see how this plays out. Now that the player's said what's on every dude's mind, we're primed for a revolution. Dudes ready to prison-riot, mount those stairs. Sheila's staring down the threat of a boner stampede.

A herd hell-bent for Cassie Wright or for the exit.

Kid dude, number 72, says to me, "I'll tell her how much I love her . . ."

Go ahead, I tell him. Fuck up Mommy's comeback. Be a needy little boy and ruin all Mommy's hard work and planning, all her training she's put into this world record. I tell the kid, Do it.

Kid 72 says, "You think I should fuck her?"

I say it's his decision.

Kid says, "I can't fuck her." Kid says, "I can't get it hard."

Halfway up the stairs, standing with numbers 247 and 354, both dudes flogging their meat, their hands stretched inside the waistband of their boxer shorts, standing here, Sheila says, "Gentlemen, would you please be patient." She says, "For Ms. Wright's well-being, we need to conduct this in a calm, organized manner."

Player dude yells, "Fuck that." He walks his plain, brown feet across the concrete to where the paper bags are stacked. With his San Diego–tanned hands, he pulls out the bag inked with "14," starts pulling out a shirt, pants, socks. Shoes that look like Armani but aren't. His skin looks like better-quality leather.

Above us on the TVs, the ugly dago police dude's jackhammering Cassie, pounding her poop chute so fast that diamonds, rubies, emeralds spill out her snatch, slot-machine style.

Kid 72 leans close, his lips by my ear and his chin almost hooked on my shoulder, and he says, "Give me a pill and I'll do it."

Fuck her? I ask. Or run up those stairs and squeal, "I love you, Mommy, I love you, I love you, Mommy, I love you . . ."?

Player dude takes out a shirt, shakes out the wrinkles. Not a real Brooks Brothers. Not even a Nordstrom. He puts his arms through each sleeve, starts doing the buttons, shooting the cuffs like this was real silk. Or even 100 percent cotton. Player dude flips the collar and slings a no-brand tie around his neck, saying, "Screw your world record, lady." Saying, "I am so, so out of here."

Above us on the TVs, the ugly dago dude, I'd bet that his under-tan goes two years back: a decent week in Mazatlán with clouds the last two days, then, a few months later, a weekend in Scottsdale, maintenance-box tanning, a week grilling in Palm Springs, a long stretch of fading, and finally a week in Palm Desert for that kind of smooth, dry finish. Not a satin-smooth

101

Ibiza tan. Or one of those coppery Mykonos fag tans. That ugly wop dude on the TV sports a greasy shine thick as cooking oil. A tan sexy as a thin coat of dirt.

Kid 72 into my ear hisses, "Give me the pill."

Sheila standing, calling the bluff, waiting.

Dudes all waiting.

Next to me, another dude's voice says, "So, Mr. Bacardi, is that Demerol in your locket?" Here's the teddy-bear dude, number 137, saying, "Are you planning an encore performance with Miss Wright?"

Kid 72 says, "What's he mean?"

Dude 137 says, "Why not drug your son? You already drugged his mother . . ."

Player dude's strapping on a knockoff Rolex President. Out of his brown grocery bag, he's fishing a bad imitation of a Hugo Boss belt I got hanging in my closet back at my apartment.

Sheila looks our way, saying, "Number 72, if you'd care to join us?"

Kid 72 whispers, "What'll I do?"

I tell him, Fuck her.

And the teddy-bear dude says, "Obey your father."

Kid 72 says, "What's that mean?"

And I shrug.

The player dude's working his cuff links, milking the job to take long as possible, his cuff links nothing better than nine-karat, even in this dim light.

Kid dude turns to the teddy-bear dude, sweat shining on the kid's face, his whites showing all around his eyes, and he says, "Give me a pill?"

Dude 137 gives the kid a long look, up and down.

Teddy-bear dude smiles and says, "What'll you pay for it?"

Kid says, "All I got is fifteen bucks in my wallet."

Still watching Sheila, her watching the player dude in their stalemate, I say money ain't what the teddy-bear dude is after. At least not fifteen bucks.

Kid says, "What, then?" He says, "Hurry."

I ask the kid if he knows the term "fluffer," what it means. I say that's what dude 137 wants.

Dude still smiling, holding his bear, says, "That's what I want."

Above us on the TVs, the camera comes in for a close-up penetration shot, and the wop dude's nut sack is pockmarked with botched electrolysis scars. Craters of the moon. Showing on a dozen TV screens, both his nuts pulled up tight under the exploded disaster of the dude's wrinkled red asshole. ·

The player dude ties his shoelaces.

And, still halfway up the stairs, Sheila yells, "Would everyone please pipe down. Just let me think . . ." She looks at her clipboard. Looks at kid 72. Looks at the player, dressed and ready to walk out. Sheila says, "Just this once . . ." She jerks her thumb at the player, saying, "Number 14, come with me." Pointing a finger at the kid, she says, "Number 72, stand down."

Dudes start back to talking, chewing their taco chips, taking leaks and not flushing the toilet. Their fingers come uncrossed. On the TVs, the ugly wop dude's sweating so hard his bronzer rolls down his cheeks in brown zebra stripes, showing the dry, flaky, fried skin underneath. To no dude in particular, pointing up at the television wop dude, I go, "Dudes, do me a favor?" I go, "Kill me if I ever look that bad."

Beside me, standing a little behind me, dude 137 says, "That was a close call . . ."

The kid, dude 72 says, "What's a fluffer?"

And Cord Cuervo says, "Dude, what are you saying?" He makes a fist and gives me a little sock in the shoulder. His bronzer glues tight to my bronzer, so he has to peel his knuckles off my shoulder skin, and Cord says, "On the TV? That *is* you, dude. From, like, five years ago."

18

Mr. 72

Mr. Bacardi stares up at the TVs they have hanging from the ceiling, showing porno, and he keeps saying, "No . . . no fucking way . . ."

Mr. Bacardi just stands in one place, staring up at the TVs, maybe using two fingers to pinch the loose skin under his jaw, pull it tight, and let go. He's staring at the movie on TV, running his fingers over his cheeks, stretching the skin back toward his ears so his wrinkles around his lips disappear, saying, "Fucking camera dude, he made me look like shit." His skin in some spots as wrinkled as my pink plastic sex surrogate, Mr. Bacardi keeps saying, "No way I look that trashed. Fucking lighting dudes . . ."

Guy 137, who used to be Dan Banyan, he holds up his autograph hound, staring it straight in the button eyes, and says, "Somebody's in denial . . ."

The headlines on those newspapers they sell at the

grocery-store checkout counter, they're true. The gossip stuff about why Dan Banyan got his TV series took off the air. That gossip they printed was real.

"I was starving. I was a starving actor," says guy 137, his head tipped back but not looking at the TVs. Instead, he's grinning at the ceiling. Laughing at the nothing there. And he says, "If anybody can identify with how Cassie Wright feels at this moment, that person is me . . .".

Above us, on the TVs, my mom's starring in *The Italian Hand Job,* where she plays an international mystery woman looking to steal the crown jewels of some place.

Mr. Bacardi sucks in his stomach and stands taller, saying, "The cheap-ass video like this, the resolution is crap." He says, "They might as well have shot this from a damned satellite."

Anger, guy 137 calls it.

"I was your age," the 137 Dan Banyan guy says and looks at me. He takes a big breath and lets it out, slow. His shoulders shrug up, high to his ears, and he says, "The finance company kept phoning me about repossessing my car. A couple late payments on my credit cards, and they jacked the interest rate up to thirty percent." His shoulders drop so his hands sag almost to his knees, and he says, "Thirty percent! On a balance of twenty-five grand, that looked like the rest of my life to pay off."

So he made a porn movie, he says.

"It can only take a moment," the 137 guy says, "to waste the rest of your life . . ."

He asks did I know a movie called *Three Days of the*

Condom. He says, "Well, it paid off my car. Didn't touch the principal on my credit card, but I got to keep my car."

He didn't figure anyone would ever see it. At the time, his acting was going nowhere. It was ten years before he got his big break in *Dan Banyan, Private Detective*.

That condom movie's been hanging over his head ever since.

"Doing an all-male gay gang-bang movie is an act of resignation," he says and waves one hand, his eyes sweeping over half the room. He says, "You and every man in here, no matter what you do up in that room, whether you tell Cassie Wright you love her, or you fuck her, or you do *both*—don't expect you'll ever get confirmed to sit on the Supreme Court."

Porn, he says, is a job you only take after you abandon all hope.

The Dan Banyan guy says half the guys here were sent by their agents to rack up some face time. He says the entire entertainment industry expects Cassie Wright to die today, and every would-be actor in town is wanting to springboard off the controversy.

"Just between you and me, kid," he says, pointing at me, then pointing at his own chest, "when your agent sends you on a look-see to fuck a dead woman, you know your career's in the toilet."

A little ways off, Mr. Bacardi digs his fingertips into the skin of his stomach, saying, "You think, if I did more hanging knee raises?" He opens both hands, turning them and looking at both sides, and says, "They have that microdermabrasion to give you young skin again." Grabbing a handful of skin above one hipbone, he says, "Maybe liposuction isn't out of the question. Calf implants. Maybe those pec implants."

The Dan Banyan guy holds up his dog, looking eye-to-eye at it, and says, "Bargaining."

On the TV screens, it's some old scene of Mr. Bacardi ramming my mom from behind. Every draw back, when he shoves his wiener in, his saggy old-man balls swing to spank my mom on her shaved taint. That no-man's-land dividing her snatch and ass.

The Dan Banyan guy, he says the only trick to starring in an all-male backdoor gang-bang movie is you have to really relax. Keep breathing, deep. You need to forget all your decades and decades of toilet training. Picture puppies and kitties. He says you kneel on the edge of a bed and five other guys come in and dork your ass a couple strokes each. Those five blow their loads across your back. Then another five come in. He really wasn't counting. Then he lost count. Taking a strong dose of Special K helped.

My mom, up those stairs, behind that locked door, under all those bright lights.

The Dan Banyan guy looks at the ceiling again and laughs, saying, "It's a lot less romantic than it might sound."

To this day, he says, you put anything up his ass and he can tell you Trojan or Sheik. Rubber versus latex versus lambskin. Without looking, just only from the feel, he says he can even name the color of the condom.

"I should do product endorsements," the Dan Banyan guy says. "I could tour as the 'Psychic Asshole' . . ."

A fluffer, he says, is somebody whose job is to blow

guys or give hand jobs to make sure they're ready to act on cue.

I don't know.

"The biggest irony is that most of the men," the Dan Banyan guy says, "in the movie with me, most of them were straight. Doing it just for the cash."

When he found that out, he says, he didn't feel half as flattered by the attention.

On the TVs, my mom is putting big fake diamonds inside her mouth. Licking them. Her lips and her snatch she has in this movie, they look nothing like what I have at home. The stuff I sent for over the Internet.

Mr. Bacardi looks at the floor, shaking his head and saying, "Who am I fooling?" Looking at his feet, only with his eyes closed, he says, "I wasted the precious gift of my life." Cupping his closed eyes with the palm of one hand, he says, "I threw away my whole precious life, trashed my life like it was nothing but a money shot."

And the Dan Banyan guy turns his head, fast, only long enough to look at Mr. Bacardi and says, "Christ! Snap out of it. Would you quit Elisabeth Kübler-Ross—ing on us!"

When he was my age, the Dan Banyan guy says, he watched Cassie Wright in *World Whore One,* he maybe even saw me get conceived, but as she took on French soldier after German soldier after doughboy, he said to himself, "Damn, I'd like to be that popular . . ." But, every casting call, he was just another young guy in a sea of young guys. TV commercials. Feature films. He never got any callbacks. Before he turned twenty-one years old, casting agents were already going on how he

109

was too old. The only last thing left for him to do was buy a bus ticket back to Oklahoma.

The Dan Banyan guy tips his bottle of pills until one rolls into the palm of his other hand. Just looking at it, he says, "My agent thinks that if I'm seen in this project it will 'out' me as being secretly straight. He's banking on *at least* bisexual." The Dan Banyan guy just looks at the blue pill sitting in his palm. His skin on his face, the blood veins swell across his dark-red forehead. His face turning the purple color of pounded meat, those blood veins twitch and squirm just inside his skin.

His agent's already got a press release printed, ready to issue. The headline across the top says "Dan Banyan Comes Out on Top!" Under that, the press release talks about the recent tragic death of one of America's topmost adult-movie stars. Most of the rest is him officially denying rumors how his massive rock-hard wiener and relentless animal ram-job is responsible for my mom being dead.

The Dan Banyan guy holds out his hand, shoving the pill at me. He says, if I want it, take it. Free of charge. I don't have to blow him or anything.

Mr. Bacardi's fingering the necklace around his neck, popping the pendant deal open and looking inside.

The pendant deal, it's a locket I've seen before. Hanging from around my mom's neck in *Blow Jobs of Madison County*. It's Cassie Wright's necklace he's wearing.

"It only takes one mistake," the Dan Banyan guy says, "and nothing else you ever do will matter." With his empty hand, he takes one of my hands. His fingers feel hot, fever-hot, and pounding with his heartbeats. He turns my hand palm-up, saying, "No matter how hard you work or how smart you become, you'll always be known for that one poor choice." He sets the blue pill on my palm, saying, "Do that one wrong thing— and you'll be dead for the rest of your life."

Mr. Bacardi's looking at a pill inside my mom's locket.

"Someone had better die today," the Dan Banyan guy says, "or I'll be headed back to Oklahoma."

And he folds my fingers shut with the little blue pill inside.

19

Mr. 137

The last time I saw
Oklahoma is the last time I *ever* want to see Oklahoma.
Picture that big circle of blue sky meeting dirt, wrapped
all the way around you. Dirt and rocks stretched from
you to the horizon. Dirt and rocks, and that sun always
up high, the noon whistle blasting at the volunteer fire
department. Dirt and rocks, and my dear, simple, good-
hearted father waiting to see me off on the Greyhound
bus bound for the temptations of the big, wicked city.

Talking to the talent wrangler, I say that if Oklahoma
the state was anything like the musical I'd still reside
there. Cowboys tap-dancing on train platforms. Gloria
Grahame. Gypsy peddlers. Elaborate dream sequences
choreographed by Martha Graham.

I lean forward and pinch, with just my fingertips, an
especially gruesome flake of dandruff off the shoulder
of the wrangler's black sweater. From the feel, a 50-
acrylic, 50-cotton blend, raglan sleeves, faux cowl neck.

Ribbed knit. Looped with snags. Awful. And I flick away the waxy flake.

On Mr. Toto, next to Gloria Grahame's fake autograph, it says, "What girl could ever say 'No' to you?!"

Watching the white flake arc and disappear in the fluttering light from the monitors, the talent wrangler says, "I use her shampoo . . ." and she tosses her head toward the movie on the screen above us, where Cassie Wright's trapped in a dystopian science-fiction future. According to the premise, war and toxic waste have killed off every other hot sex goddess except her. As the last surviving hottie, she has to wear crippling thong underwear, a push-up bra, and high heels, then fuck or suck off every guy in the evil fascist, quasi-religious, theocratic, Old Testament–inspired government. The movie's called *The Handmaid's Tail*.

A classic of social-commentary porn.

"It's how I got this job," the wrangler says. "During my pitch meeting, Ms. Wright smelled my hair."

Me, too, I say, and touch the hairs combed across my own scalp.

"I kind of guessed," she says, frowning. "Either that or you're having chemotherapy or you have some terrible, fatal disease."

No, I tell her. Just the shampoo.

"You're wrong," she says.

Okay, I tell her, maybe I bottomed for an army of strangers in some forgettable gang-bang flick, but I do not have some terrible disease. Buried somewhere in the papers on her clipboard, she can dig out my STD report.

"No," she says. Reading over the names and inscriptions scribbled on Mr. Toto's white canvas skin, the wrangler says, "It wasn't Martha Graham. It was Agnes de Mille."

On Mr. Toto, I spelled her autograph with only one "L." "Agnes de Mile." A dead giveaway.

That's okay, I tell her. In my life, I've been wrong about almost everything.

You'd better believe I didn't give them the full story about me, my beloved father, and all of that lovely, lovely Oklahoma lying flat, as far as the eye could see. No, you can ask, but I'm saving myself for Charlie Rose. Barbara Walters. Larry King. Or Oprah Winfrey. No one except a certified talk-show god is going to dissect my private parts.

Waiting for that Greyhound bus, my father kept telling me to write. As soon as I got settled in California, I should write them a postcard, telling him and my mother where to send my mail. Of course he told me to phone, to telephone collect if I had to. And right away, once I arrived in Los Angeles, just so my mother wouldn't worry.

Fathers. Mothers. With all their caring and attention. They will fuck you up, every time.

The talent wrangler stands still, her shoulders pinned back so I can pinch the waxy white flakes off her sweater. In her eyes dance tiny screens of Cassie Wright, reflected. As the last hottie in the sci-fi future, for her own protection, Cassie can only venture out in public wearing a billowing cloak and wide hat. Almost a nun's habit, only red.

A voice says, "Make sure he wears a rubber, Sheila." A man's voice. Branch Bacardi's stopped next to us, his stomach sucked back to his spine but skin still slopped out over the elastic waistband of his red satin prize-fighter shorts.

Sheila doesn't say a word. She won't even give him a look.

Bacardi hooks his thumb at me, saying, "You're barking up the wrong team, honey."

Bacardi folds his arms over his shaved chest. He smiles, running his tongue over his top teeth, winks, and says, "But if you want babies inside you, I'm your man."

And the black poly-cotton rib-knit awfulness of the talent wrangler's sweater, it shudders. Her shoulders shudder and her eyes close as she says, "Rapist."

In Oklahoma, my high school graduation had been Saturday night, and this was Monday morning. One minute I'm walking the football field, wearing my black cap and gown, accepting my diploma from Superintendent Frank Reynolds. The next minute I'm standing next to my suitcase, a present mail-ordered for graduation. Both my father and I squinting down the road. Looking for that bus, my father says, "You write if you meet any girl, special."

A couple dandruff flakes after Branch Bacardi's walked away, the talent wrangler says, "He pressured her to get an abortion. Said he'd pay for it. Said a baby would ruin her tits, end her career in movies."

The wrangler says she needs to collect the brown paper bags for the three men who are with Cassie Wright, on set. She needs to take them their clothes and shoes.

Across the room, the young actor looks at the pill cupped in the palm of his hand.

Just teasing, I ask why we never see anybody once they're called to the set. Is this some mass black-widow-spider snuff movie? Does somebody on set kill each of the six hundred actors the moment after they ejaculate?

Just joking, I mean.

But the wrangler only looks at me for one, two, three flakes of dandruff, my fingertips pinching them and flicking them away. Four, five, six flakes later, she says, "Yes. This is actually an elaborate scheme to steal men's used clothing . . ."

Pinching white flakes, I ask the wrangler why she doesn't just renumber an actor and run him through the set several times. They could shoot just his arm, each time with a different number. That way, the young man, number 72, could leave. The production wouldn't depend on keeping everyone happy and trapped here.

One hand holding her clipboard so the bottom edge is braced against her stomach, her free hand slips the thick black felt-tipped pen from the clip. The wrangler waves the pen next to her face, beside her eyes, and says, "Indelible ink."

That Monday morning in Oklahoma, squinting into the sun and the distance, his eyes watering against the wavy smell of the hot blacktop, my father says, "You do know, don't you? About being with a gal?" He says, "I mean, about protecting yourself?"

I told him I knew. I know.

And he said, "Have you?"

Worn a rubber? I asked. Or been with a girl?

116

And he laughed, slapping one hand on his thigh, puffing up dust from his jeans, he said, "Why else would you wear a rubber if you ain't been with a gal?"

Oklahoma ringed around us, the world spread out from the spot we're standing, the gravel side of the highway, only him and me, I told my father I was never going to meet the right girl.

And he said, "Don't you say that." Still watching the horizon, he said, "You just got to encourage yourself some."

That black pen, the wrangler says, you can't wash it off. You can't scratch it off. Once she writes a number on you, it's permanent as a tattoo for roughly the lifespan of a full bar of soap in your shower.

Sliding the pen back under the clip of her clipboard, she says, "I hope you have a lot of long-sleeved shirts."

The rocks and sun. The Greyhound bus not here. All my clothes folded and layered in my suitcase. I should've shut up. Changed the subject of conversation to the weather report, maybe the bushel price of winter wheat. We could've run out the clock talking about Mrs. Wellton, who runs the post office, and her spastic colon. Another line of dialogue, about the new Massey tractors versus the John Deere, a little back-and-forth about how wet last summer turned out, and both of us would be a ton happier right now.

That Greyhound bus still somewhere under the horizon.

But wouldn't you know it? I fucked everything up. My last ten minutes before leaving home, I told my father I was an Oklahomo.

Talking to the talent wrangler, I swallow another little pill. Sweat slides down from my hairline to my eyebrows, down my temples to my cheeks. Sweat hangs, swings from my earlobes. Drops fall, splashing dark spots around my feet. The skin of my neck burns, hot.

The talent wrangler says, "Lay off those pills." She says, "You don't look so healthy."

I tell her I'm not sick.

The bus still somewhere else, my father said, "It's a misunderstanding, you being how you figure." He spits in the dust, the gravel and dust of the road's shoulder, and says, "It's on account of somebody doing something evil to you when you was little."

Somebody diddled me.

I ask, Who?

"You don't got to know names," my father says. "Only know you ain't naturally the way you figure."

I asked, Who diddled me?

My father only shook his head.

Then it's a lie, I tell him. He's lying out of hope I'll change. He's making up a story to confuse me. Inventing some reason why I can't just be happy how I am. Nobody around here's a child molester.

But he only shakes his head, saying, "Ain't no lie." Saying, "I wish it was."

The bus still not here.

"Relax, dude," a voice says. Here in the basement, Branch Bacardi says, "You die in there, pitch yourself a stroke or a heart attack, and they'll just roll you on your back and let Cassie ride a reverse cowgirl on your hard, dead dick."

Walking away, he says, "Nothing if not a numbers game, that's what today is."

118

Pinching white flakes off the wrangler's sweater, I say how one gruesome possibility is that I allowed fifty or more strange men to fuck my ass just to make my father wrong . . .

My worst fear is that I got fucked by the equivalent of five baseball teams just to prove my father wasn't a pervert.

The same heartbeat when the bus popped up on the horizon, my father said, "You got to trust me."

I say he's lying. My knees bent low enough my hand could grip the handle of my suitcase. My legs stand. My mouth says he's lying to try and keep me straight.

The bus, bigger with every word.

He says, "Would you believe if I told you who done it?"

Who diddled me when I was a baby.

My other hand, holding my bus ticket, shaking.

The bus almost here, that last little while of us talking in Oklahoma, my father says, "It was me."

It was him diddled me.

Talking to the talent wrangler, picking flakes off her sweater, by accident instead of a pill I slip a flake between my lips. Her dead skin, chewy with grease or wax. I spit it out.

Hanging over us on the monitors, Cassie Wright tears her sci-fi nun's habit into long strips she begins to braid with pastel-pink-and-yellow bras and thongs, tying together a rope she can climb to escape from her window.

I ask the wrangler can I pick the flakes out of her hair.

And the wrangler shrugs, saying, "Only the ones that show . . ."

In Oklahoma, the Greyhound bus pulls up to us, me and my father in the flat center of our state, and he says, "It was a one-time mistake, boy." He says, "But don't you make it last the rest of your life."

The air brakes set. The metal door folds open. One, two, three steps, and my feet stand on board, my hand getting my ticket taken by the driver. My lips saying, "Los Angeles."

My father down below, calling, "Write like you promised." Saying, "Don't you live what's not your fault, boy."

My ears hearing all that.

The talent wrangler watches Branch Bacardi, her eyes attached to him. Only looking away when he looks back at her, she says, "Yeah, parents will always fuck you up . . ."

My feet walked me down the aisle of the Greyhound bus, all the way to the back. My butt sat me in a seat.

My butt's accomplished a lot since then.

My butt's a movie star.

Only wouldn't you know it? I never did write home.

20

Sheila

In 1944, while she was filming the movie *Kismet,* Marlene Dietrich bronzed her legs with copper paint. Lead-based copper-colored paint. The lead leached into her skin. Almost poisoned her to death. Ms. Wright tells me this while I stir the wax melting in a double boiler.

Ms. Wright, she's shucking off her long-sleeved top, her jeans and panties. Naked, Ms. Wright bends to spread a bath towel across the top of her kitchen table. Her two-room apartment, the bare walls busy with nail holes. Not a stick of furniture except a soiled white sofa that folds out to make a bed. Two kitchen chairs bent out of chrome, and a table to match. Ms. Wright spreads a second and third towel across the table. Spreads another until the towels add up to a thick pad.

The cabinets are empty. Inside her fridge, you'd maybe find some takeout, wrapped in tinfoil from the

121

Greek place on the first floor. Balanced on the tank of her toilet, her last roll of tissue.

Sitting her bare-naked ass on the edge of the kitchen table, Ms. Wright says that the actor Lucille Ball always refused cosmetic surgery. No face-lifts for Lucy. Instead, she grew out the hair at her temples, long thick strands of hair that hung over each ear. Before she made any public appearance, shot any television or movie work, Lucy would wind those long locks of hair around wooden toothpicks. With a wig cap pulled tight over the crown of her head, Lucy would pull each toothpick up and backward, stretching and lifting the sagging skin of each cheek. Snag the toothpicks into the mesh of the wig cap, then pull on a red bouffant wig to hide the whole mess. Past a certain age, anytime you see Lucille Ball on television reruns, mugging and bawling for laughs, smiling and looking wonderful for her age, that woman is in agony.

True fact, according to Ms. Wright.

Nodding at the boxes stacked in the living room, boxes marked "Charity" or "Trash," I ask if she's planning a trip.

And Ms. Wright scoots her butt back on the towels. Hands clamped around the edge of the table, to keep the towels in place, she slides back until she's sitting. Centered on the towels, Ms. Wright leans back to rest on her elbows. Draws up both her feet to rest on the edge of the table. All of her naked. Knees spread wide, bent to give her frog legs, she says, "Am I going somewhere?"

Her fingernails pick around in her bush, pluck out a

curly gray hair, and Ms. Wright drops the hair to the floor, saying, "Don't let's be coy, okay?"

She says the actor Barbara Stanwyck used to spread Elmer's white glue on her own face. The same way we'd spread that glue on our hands in grade school. The lactic acid loosened any dull, dead skin cells, and picking, pulling, peeling off the mask of dried glue would vacuum out her pores and yank stray hairs.

Ms. Wright says the movie star Tallulah Bankhead used to collect eggshells and grind them into a coarse powder, then mix this with a glass of water and drink it. The crushed eggshells rubbed, roughed, ruined her throat just enough to give her a deep, sultry speaking voice. Rumor is, Lauren Bacall did the same trick.

Ms. Wright eyes my hair. She tosses her chin and says to grind an aspirin and mix that in a little shampoo. Wash my hair with the mix, and it will fix any dandruff.

Me? I just keep stirring the wax.

And Ms. Wright says, her legs spread in the middle of the kitchen table, "Didn't your momma teach you anything?"

Marilyn Monroe, she says, used to cut the heel of one shoe, to make her one leg shorter, to make her ass grind together as she walked.

The best way to fade a hickey is with regular toothpaste. To shrink swollen eyes, lie down with a slice of raw potato over each. The potato's alpha-lipoic acid stops inflammation. Exfoliate your face with a baking-soda scrub, and never use soap.

The wax, I tell her, is ready. Not too hot or too thick.

On the stove, one pot of the soft wax, the yellow kind, that you boil in its own little can. Another pot holds a bag of those pellets from France, identical to a bag of split peas, only dark blue. Hard wax, melted to make a dark-blue paste.

Ms. Wright asks, "You cut the muslin?"

The roll of muslin tape, wide and white as a roll of cash-register or adding-machine tape, I've already cut a batch of it into small squares.

Watching me dip a wooden stick, what doctors used to call a tongue depressor, watching me dip and swirl the stick in the pot of yellow wax, Ms. Wright says to start with the dark-blue wax. The hard wax is easier to control. The dark-blue French wax gives you a better outline. Better control around the sensitive edge of things.

Watching me loop a glob of hot dark-blue wax and turn to lean in between her knees, Ms. Wright says how Dolores del Rio used to daub on the powder of grape Jell-O mix to stain her nipples dark. The better to show through clothes. Rita Hayworth used strawberry Jell-O mix to dye hers bright pink.

The pinup girl, Betty Grable, sprayed her bare butt and breasts with hairspray until they were wet. That way the top and bottom of her swimsuit stayed glued where she wanted. Hairspray inside your high heels works the same way.

Spread on the table, Ms. Wright's gray muff. Bushy blond with gray roots. The pink line of her episiotomy scar trailing a tiny ways out the bottom. Wiping the wooden stick, I smear the blue wax, dragging the hot wax with the growth pattern of the hair.

Her leg muscles jump, spasm, cramp into patterns

124

under her skin. Eyes squeezed shut. Ms. Wright says how the pud-pounder Lon Chaney used to boil eggs. Playing the Phantom of the Opera, Chaney used to bring hard-boiled eggs to the film set. Before shooting, he'd peel an egg and carefully pull the rubbery white membrane off the egg white. To look blind, Chaney would spread this egg membrane over his iris. A fake cataract. Bacteria collected under the membrane, and Chaney lost sight in that eye.

True fact.

With the tongue depressor, I loop up another gob of hot wax. Smear it to cover a little more of Ms. Wright's bush.

To kill the pain, the tearing, searing, scalding pain when you yank off the hair, Ms. Wright says, most technicians press the spot. Press hard and it deadens the nerve endings. But the better way, she says, is to slap. Real experts pull off the wax, yank it hard, and slap the bare spot. Hard.

She says you should always shave your legs in the morning. At night they're a teeny bit swollen, so you'll never get the whole hair. By morning, you'll have stubble.

Looping up another hot gob of wax, I ask why she had the baby she gave away. Why didn't she just, you know, terminate? Why go through all the hassle of giving birth if she wasn't going to keep it? And, leaning over that chrome kitchen table, I paint another steaming dark-blue stripe between her legs.

To exfoliate, Ms. Wright says to scrub with cold, used coffee grounds. The tannic acid gently peels off dead skin. To hide cellulite, press the skin with a layer

125

of warm coffee grounds for ten minutes. Your dimpled thighs will look better instantly, but only for the next twelve hours.

She says the way her baby was conceived was so awful, such a betrayal, that she wanted just one good thing to come of it.

Ms. Wright nods her head at the next steaming glob of molten wax and says, "If you puts a knife under the kitchen table, I hears it cuts the pain in two . . ."

In adult features, she says, the close-up of the erection inserted in the orifice is called the "meat shot." Her eyes still closed, teeth clenched, her fingers balled into fists as the wax dries and sweat soaks into the folded towel, Ms. Wright says, "Mr. DeMille, I'm ready for my meat shot . . ."

Says to rip off the wax, pulling in the direction opposite the hair's growth pattern. Says to pull fast and slap the bare spot.

The church smell of burning candles. A birthday-cake smell, before you make your wish and blow. From her pussy, the bakery smell of warm bread.

Through her gritted teeth, she says, "I didn't set out to be a porn star . . ."

Ms. Wright says a classic French trick is to soak a washcloth with cold milk and hold it on your face for several minutes. Next, soak a washcloth in hot tea and cover your face. The cold protein of the milk and the hot antioxidants of the tea will increase the blood circulation in your skin, and you'll glow.

Trails of sweat braid down her bare thighs. Soak darker spots into the pad of layered towels. Ms. Wright says, "Did you love your momma?"

And I pick at the edge of the blue wax. Peel a little up from the skin. Yank away a long stretch of the stiff dark-blue. Rip off a strip of blond carpet with gray tips. Slap the skin, hard.

This must hurt, because Ms. Wright's eyes brim with tears.

From the waist down, reduced to a little girl. Smooth as a baby's bottom.

Spots of blood well up from everywhere. Every hair follicle a pin-spot of red.

I slap again, to kill the pain, and a tear mixed with mascara tips out one eye and rolls a black stripe down Ms. Wright's face. So I slap harder, leaving both of us spattered in her blood.

21

Mr. 600

Teddy-bear dude and Sheila look thick together. Cozy. Dude's touching her tits and hair. Sheila talking shit to him about me. Both of them looking at me. Pointing fingers at me. Talking their shit.

Television dude keeps touching his own head, shedding hairs. The blood veins ballooning on his face, all branchy, red and shit. His eyeballs all pug-dogged, bulging and ready to roll down his cheeks. His eyes looking red with blood veins, blinking with water. Sweat washing his hairline, flat against his neck and forehead.

Teddy-bear dude's not doing so well.

Symptoms not even his glazed, dark Palm Springs tan can cover.

Those tests that Sheila had dudes take, the clinic reports most dudes had to bring, none of that's foolproof.

Rubbers break. Rumor is, even rubbers aren't thick enough to block a virus.

Walking, I'm pacing same as those tigers at the zoo, weaving between dudes. Making big circles going around the room, I'm navigating through clouds of baby-oil stink and Stetson cologne, careful to keep from skidding on the oily footprints left by dudes trying to shine.

Teddy-bear dude's not getting porked by a million diseased, sex-hound dudes, then passing his problems on to me. Sure, I may be anchor dude 600, but I'm not riding sloppy seconds after him. It's okay he kills a babe who wants to die, but he's not killing me. Not just so he's got work for the next couple years.

Dudes tell a joke. They say, "How many queer fuck films end as snuff films?" The answer being, "You wait long enough—all of them!"

That joke . . . that's not a joke.

Sheila and the teddy-bear dude still looking at me. Talking their shit.

A ways off, the kid 72 keeps looking in his hand, rolling around the wood pill.

On the TVs, Cassie is naked and sliding down some kind of tangled-up bras and shit, falling out a window, and landing on some grass, outside, at night. Wearing nothing but spike heels and dangle earrings, she takes off running with a bunch of those Doberman pointy-eared dogs chasing her and loud sirens wailing. Searchlights sweep over the grass and night and stuff.

Teddy-bear dude laughs. Sheila laughs. Both of them looking at me.

No, I ain't as young as I've been, but I don't have to take this amount of disrespect. My name's attached some of the financing for this project. My hard years helped bankroll the taco chips and shit they're chowing down. The rental on this place. Paid for that bed dudes are up there busting. All that seems to indicate I got some measure of respect coming to me.

Kid 72, the little dummy stands there looking at the pill in his hand, looking at Cassie running ahead of those barking dogs.

I stop next to the kid. I go, "Hey, you come here today planning to die?"

I go, "Of course you didn't. Me, neither."

I go, "Teddy-bear Dan Banyan dude's going to snuff us both."

I go how I got a plan, and for him to follow me. The two of us walk, innocentlike, over by where the dude and Sheila stand, them talking. Her holding her clipboard. Him holding that bear with Britney Spears' name on it.

My bronzer, I tell Sheila how it's started to cover up the number on my arm, and I ask can I borrow her pen, to do a quick touch-up on my "600."

Sheila looks at me, her mouth jerking at one corner to show her teeth on that side. The holes of her nose dialed so big the air tunnels into her head look pink as seashells all the ways back to her brain. Sheila tugs the pen out from the top of her clipboard and holds it across to me.

I take it and go, "Thanks, honey."

Sheila says nothing. Her and the teddy-bear dude

not saying a word. Not laughing. Their eyes and trash talk waiting for me to walk off.

To fool them, I take a couple steps, the kid in tow. Both of us, we swing around behind Sheila. Casuallike. I pop the cap off the pen, write a new "600" on my arm, over the old number. Switch hands and write on my other arm.

The kid's looking at his mom trying to climb a big tree, naked in high heels, the scene shot from a really low angle, with dogs barking around the tree and security guards catching up. Cassie's thong tan-line, ghosted at the edges with a hint of Acapulco sun, a couple weeks of beige Monterey tanning bordered with the hard red leftover from some lost weekend in Tijuana.

With just one step, I'm against the back of the teddy-bear dude, looping my free hand under his arm from behind. That hand of mine snakes around to the back of his neck, cupping my fingers over the thin hair in back of his head. Pulling back, I hold him in a half nelson, his loose hand slapping. Dude's feet slip on the smeared baby-oil floor, kicking without traction, as I reach the felt-tip pen into his face and write what I planned. Three big letters across his TV-star forehead. My muscles relax, and he slips out of the hold, spinning to face me.

The whole deal faster than the words to describe it.

My whole entire front, my chest and arms and abs, slimy with the dude's sweat.

The teddy-bear dude, beet red, looking at the pen in my hand, he goes, "What did you write?"

Both his hands jump to his forehead, rubbing and

131

looking for black on his fingertips. Scrubbing with both hands, he goes, "You wrote 'FAG,' didn't you?" Looking at kid 72, he goes, "Did he write 'FAG'?"

The kid just shakes his head.

The teddy-bear dude looks at Sheila.

And Sheila goes, "Worse."

Me tossing the pen back to Sheila, I go, "He wants publicity? That should get him some publicity." Sheila lets the pen land on the concrete next to her shoes. Next to the pen, the dude's dropped his teddy bear he's always holding, the ink writing smudged and blurred, dissolved with the baby oil on the floor.

Teddy-bear dude's spitting on his fingers, rubbing his forehead. "You," he goes, "you raped this kid's mother. You drugged her and ruined her life."

Kid 72 goes, "How's that?"

Sheila lifts one hand to look at her wristwatch, and she goes, "Gentlemen, may I have your attention . . ."

No duh, every dude looks up. Dudes look to hear better. Arms reach up to kill the sound on some of the televisions. The barking dogs and sirens, gone.

The teddy-bear dude huffs off to the bathroom, elbowing dudes out of his way. His bare feet slapping the floor.

"I need the following performers," Sheila goes, looking down at her list.

To me, kid 72 goes, "Who'd you drug?"

Yelling back at us, yelling big in all the quiet, the teddy-bear dude goes, "Wake up, you idiot. That bastard's your father."

"Number 569 . . . ," Sheila calls out. "Number 337 . . ."

132

In the bathroom doorway, the teddy-bear dude shoulders his way past the dudes there, slippery with baby oil, froze as statues to hear better.

Sheila stoops to grab the pen at her feet. Standing, she goes, "And number 137 . . ."

To the kid, I go, "I'm not dying 'cause of today."

Kid 72 leans over to grab the teddy bear where it's landed on the greasy floor.

And in the bathroom, looking in the mirror over the little sink, the teddy-bear dude starts to scream.

22

Mr. 72

The girl with the stopwatch keeps calling the Dan Banyan guy until he comes out the bathroom door with water running down his face, soap foaming along his hairline, with what's left of his hair pasted down flat to the sides of his head. The clipboard girl's standing at the top of the stairs, outlined against the open door. Those lights on the set too bright to look straight at. From behind her, the light's dancing around her dark shape. The girl keeps calling for Dan Banyan by his number, 137, until he starts up the stairs, still scrubbing wads of wet paper towel against his forehead.

Every guy's looking someplace else, from the brightness and the sight of Detective Dan Banyan sniffing, mopping his eyes with both hands, his shoulders rolled to the front and shaking, his mouth saying, ". . . it's not true . . ." between big breaths that jerk and catch in his throat.

To look someplace else, I stoop down, reach down with one hand, and grab his autograph dog where it's landed on the floor. Only it's too late, oil off some guy's feet or spilled soda or cold piss tracked out of the bathroom, something's soaked into the stuffed dog and blurred the names that used to be Liza Minnelli and Olivia Newton-John. The dog's skin all blotched and bruised with dark shapes and spots.

With nobody looking, the 137 Dan Banyan guy disappears into the light, his forehead still wrecked from Mr. Bacardi drawing the word "HIV" there.

On his dog, you can't tell anymore how much Julia Roberts loves him. The canvas body feels wet, cold, and sticky, and where I touch its skin my fingers turn black.

Talking to Mr. Bacardi, I say, Dan Banyan's going to want his dog. I say, So my mom can autograph it.

Mr. Bacardi only just watches the door after it's shut, the top of the stairs, where Dan Banyan's gone. Still looking at that door, Mr. Bacardi says, "Kid, your old man, did he ever have that classic sex talk with you?"

I tell him he's not my dad. My holding the dog out to him, he won't take it.

Still watching that door, Mr. Bacardi says, "Best advice my old man ever gave me was"—and he smiles, his eyes still on that door—"if you shave the hair back from around the base of your dick, hard or soft, you'll look two inches longer." Mr. Bacardi shuts his eyes, shakes his head. He opens his eyes, looking at me now. Looking at the dog in my hand, he says, "You want to be a hero?"

On the dog, the wet parts keep dissolving words,

turning Meryl Streep into more mixed red and blue ink, purple bruises the color of blood blisters, the track marks and cancer my adopted dad would paint on an itty-bitty train-model needle freak.

Spreading the fingers of one hand, waving his hand to show me the whole underground basement, Mr. Bacardi says, "You want to save every dude down here?"

I only want to save my mom.

"Then," Mr. Bacardi says, "give your mom this." And he taps one finger against the gold heart hanging from the chain around his neck. The chain stretches tight, stiff as wire, to fit around his big neck, and the heart sits up against his throat, so tight that when he talks, every word makes the gold heart rattle and jump. "Give her this," Mr. Bacardi says, making the heart dance, "and you'll walk out of here rich."

Fat chance.

By mistake, I told my adopted folks about the movie shooting here today, and right away their boots were on my throat, saying how if I even left the house today they'd disown me. They'd change the locks and call the Goodwill to send a truck for my clothes and bed and stuff. My bank account I have, it needs their signature for me to take out any money, since it's supposed to pay for college. After my adopted mom told about catching me with that secondhand Cassie Wright inflatable sex surrogate, that was their condition for letting me have a savings account. Any money I got paid mowing lawns or walking dogs, I had to put into that account, where I can't spend it without their say-so.

Telling this to Mr. Bacardi, I'm working my way

136

toward the food they got laid out. The dips and candy. After buying these roses for my mom, I don't have the price of a large pizza. Filling up on taco chips and cheese popcorn, I say how my plan was to show up today and rescue her, save and support my mom so she's not forced to do porno, only now I can't even buy my dinner.

Smearing cheese log on crackers, dipping celery sticks in ranch dressing, I keep talking, telling Mr. Bacardi that what's in that brown paper bag with my number, 72, that's everything I own in the world.

Balancing the bouquet of roses, I'm spearing toothpicks into little wieners.

Holding the wet autograph dog under one arm, I'm wiping barbecue sauce on garlic bread.

Mr. Bacardi's eyeing me. He's making wrinkles with his forehead and a frown with his mouth. He reaches one hand to behind his neck. Then reaches back with his other, both hands touching the back of his neck, the hair of his armpits showing, gray stubble. "Hold on," he says, and the chain around his neck goes loose, comes apart. Mr. Bacardi dangles the gold heart, swinging from the chain hanging from his hand. He holds the heart out to me and says, "Now you have this: your key to fame and fortune."

Swinging the heart so it flashes in the TV light, he says, "Imagine never having to work another day in your life. Dude, can you? Picture being rich and famous from today forward."

My adopted mom, I tell him, she's such a hypocrite. The day she caught me with the sex surrogate, she'd come home from her cake-decorating workshop. Her and my adopted dad sleep in rooms other than each other's, since forever. My adopted mom stops me from surfing the Web, afraid I'll get more corrupted, and her cake-decorating workshop hires a visit from a baker who does erotic cakes, those sex cakes of naked people for a joke, where, instead of asking for a corner piece or a frosting flower, everybody jokes they want the left testicle. Such a hypocrite. After that, she's in the kitchen practicing boiled-icing scrotums and lemon-curd assholes, mixing food coloring to make clits and nipples. Wasting gallons of buttercream frosting to squeeze out row after row of foreskins on sheets of wax paper. You open our fridge, and inside you'll find sheets of labia, leftover lengths of thigh or butt cheek, same as the kitchen of Jeffrey Dahmer.

My adopted dad would be in the basement, detailing tiny German nurses, nail-filing their breasts down flat, painting their fingernails dirty, and blacking out their teeth to make underage prostitutes. My adopted mom would be dyeing shredded coconut to make pubic hairs, or twisting the end of a pastry bag to pipe red veins down the side of a devil's-food erection.

The wet autograph dog leaks a trickle of watery ink down my side, my leg, the inside of my arm.

And Mr. Bacardi says, "Take it." Holding the gold heart in my face, he says, "Look inside."

My fingers sticky with powdered sugar and doughnut jelly, I'm still holding the little pill Dan Banyan gave me, cupped in one hand, the drug for when I need to get my wiener hard. While I'm juggling the bouquet

of roses, the wood pill, and the wet dog, my fingernails
pry at the gold heart until it pops open. On the inside,
a baby looks out, just a squashed wad of skin, bald, the
lips puckered, wrinkled as the inflatable sex surrogate.
Me. I'm this baby.

The heart still warm from Mr. Bacardi's throat. Slippery with his baby oil.

On the other inside sits a little pill.

Just a plain little pill. Inside the heart.

"Potassium cyanide," Mr. Bacardi says.

He says to hide it in the paper funnel of my flowers.

"Cassie's a born masochist," he says. "It's the greatest
gift a son could give her . . ."

I don't know.

She wants it, he says. She begged him to bring it,
even gave him her necklace to sneak it in here.

Mr. Bacardi says, "Say it's from Irwin, and she'll
know."

I ask him, Irwin?

"That was me," he says. "It used to be my name."

He says to give it to her and she'll die and I'll walk
out of here a rich dude. I'll have enough money, I won't
need a family, I won't need friends. If you're rich enough,
Mr. Bacardi says, you don't need anybody.

The baby inside, all wrinkled and lumpy. The smooth
little pill.

What Cassie Wright didn't want versus what she
does want.

What she threw away versus what she's asked for.

Mr. Bacardi says, "Your ma's nothing if not strong-
minded. She wanted liposuction, I paid for it. She

wanted boob implants, I paid. All that money to suck out fat and inject plastic."

The baby's picture, she's wore it around her neck for most of her life.

Mr. Bacardi says, "It was Cassie wanted to shoot a porn loop to escape her folks' house. Cassie asked could I score her something to help relax."

The baby's nose, my nose. The fat chin, my chin. The squinty eyes, mine.

My mom swallows this pill, maybe only bites down on it, and her muscles paralyze. She can't breathe on account of her diaphragm's stopped, and her skin turns blue. No pain or blood, and she's just dead.

My mom's just dead. This here's the last world-record gang-bang movie ever. She's a dead hero, and we all go into the history books.

"Added benefit," Mr. Bacardi says, "nobody has to follow the diseased teddy-bear dude." He says, "You'll be saving lives, kid."

All I need to do is hide the cyanide in my flowers, give her the flowers, and say they're from Irving.

"Irwin," says Mr. Bacardi.

I say we've got a big problem.

The wet autograph dog, it's printed the name Cloris Leachman on my side skin, only backwards. Next to that's printed "You mean the world to me," only in reverse.

"I swear," Mr. Bacardi says, "it's what she wants most."

That baby looking up at both of us.

And I say no. The problem is the light, the dim light down here. Cupped in the palm of my hand, the cyanide

and the wood pill, I can't tell which is which. What's
sex and what's death—I can't tell the difference.

I ask which one to give her.

And Mr. Bacardi leans in to look, both of us breathing hot, damp air into my open hand.

23

Mr. 137

The talent wrangler does her best to show me the door. A couple laughs, not two puffs on a cigarette after I ejaculate across Cassie Wright's lovely breasts, my sperm still warm and crawling around, and the wrangler's shoving a paper bag full of clothes into my arms. She's telling me to get dressed. Me, I'm telling Ms. Wright how moved I was by her performance as a struggling, unstoppable teacher yearning to make a difference among the disadvantaged students of a gritty inner-city school. She was inspired. Just inspired. Her character's vulnerability and determination, she was the best part of watching *The Asshole Jungle*.

Later released as *How Reamed Was My Valley*.

Later re-released as *Inside Miss Jean Brodie*.

Ms. Wright squealed. She actually squealed over the fact I knew the film. That I knew all her films, from *Angels with Dirty Places* to *Sperms of Endearment*.

Her favorite color is fuchsia. Her favorite scent: sandalwood. Ice cream: French vanilla. Pet peeve: shops that ask you to check your bags as you enter.

Sniffing my hair, she squealed again.

The two of us, we chatted about cotton sheets versus poly-cotton blends. We gossiped about Kate Hepburn, dyke or not? Ms. Wright says: Definitely. We nattered about our mothers. Through all our small talk, I'm pumping away, in her vagina, in her bottom, in her hand, between her breasts. Us having our little hen party, just yak-yak-yakking away, and my erection's going in and out, in and out.

The talent wrangler stands next to the bed, just off camera, holding a stopwatch in one hand.

Wouldn't you know it? Ms. Wright and I, we're barely into the subject of favorite diets when the wrangler presses the top of the watch with her thumb and says, "Time."

Next, I'm holding a bag of clothes, being herded toward an open door filled with sunlight. My briefs are still looped around my ankles, so I'm waddling, my erection swinging in front of me like a blind man's cane, and the talent wrangler has the nerve to say, "Thank you for coming . . ."

One shove from me standing in the alley, naked, my skin still hot from the set lights, I look in the bag and see an off-brand acrylic men's two-button rugby shirt with a one-piece collar and contrasting stripes, banded sleeves, and not the slightest hint of taper, and I put my foot down.

These are not my clothes. Yes, the bag's marked "137," my number, but my clothes, my shoes, Mr. Toto, they're all still back in the green room. The wrangler needs to let me backtrack. She doesn't let me go back and look, I tell the wrangler, and I'm calling the police. My bare foot tap-tap-tapping the concrete hallway one step from the alley, I wait.

And, looking at her watch, the wrangler says, "Okay." She says, "Fine." She sighs and says, "Come back and look."

At the top of the stairs, looking down on the few actors still waiting, I say, Gentlemen. Wearing only my briefs, bowing from the waist, I spread both arms and say, You are no longer looking at a perfect Kinsey Six.

Mr. Toto tucked under his arm, a potato chip stopped halfway to his mouth, the young actor 72 says, "Is she dead?"

Branch Bacardi says, "What was the point?" Tapping a finger on his forehead, he says, "They couldn't shoot your face. That means no publicity."

To draw out the moment, I take a step down the stairs. I take another step. On the monitors, Cassie Wright takes the hand of a deaf and blind actor. She folds his fingers into a pattern and presses his hand into her crotch, saying, "Water . . ." My favorite scene from *The Miracle Sex Worker*. With another step, I take another moment. A long pause of quiet as I stroll across the concrete to where Bacardi stands. Wordless, I nod to accept Mr. Toto from the young man.

Still silent, I smile and lift one hand to brush back the hair from my forehead, the skin revealed, and written across it: "How I loVe U . . ." inscribed and autographed by Cassie Wright.

To the young actor 72 I say, "Her own idea." Patting the fingers of one hand against my lips, I blow a kiss toward the stairs and the set, saying, "Your mother is a bona fide angel."

His shaved chest bare, empty, Branch Bacardi rolls his eyes. The locket is gone, and he says, "So you managed to fuck her."

Not to brag, but I performed so well that I'm beginning to wonder if my poor dear father in Oklahoma isn't in fact the pervert he confessed to be.

Actor 72 makes a fist around something—the locket, with its chain dangling between his fingers. He looks at Bacardi and says, "I'm starting to wonder the same deal."

From her perch at the top of the stairs, the wrangler shouts, "Gentlemen, may I have your attention . . ."

The row of bags line the wall, mine still among them. The room's grown darker since I left. The ambient light from the monitors, less bright.

Actor 72 says, "Mr. Banyan?" He opens his fist and lifts it to under my nose. Two pills rest in the hollow of his palm, and he asks, "Which of these did you give me for an erection?"

"May I have the following performers," the wrangler shouts.

Both pills look the same.

"Number 471 . . ." the wrangler says. "Number 268 . . ."

I blink. Squint. I lean forward too far, too fast, and knock my face against the actor's hand. "Hold still . . ." I say. With my right eye shut, I'm blind. Open or shut,

145

I can't see anything out of my left eye. Wouldn't you know? That mini-stroke or whatnot the wrangler and Bacardi were harping about.

This moment, when Branch Bacardi's under my thumb, this magic shining moment when he's my bitch, I'm not letting him be right. I stumble until my hip brushes the edge of a buffet table; not seeing, I reach down and grab the first snack my fingers touch. I pop it into my mouth and start chewing. Relaxed. Nonchalant.

The wrangler says, ". . . and number 72."

The young actor nods at his hand. He says, "Hurry, please. Which one do I take?"

On the young actor's hand I smell cheddar cheese, garlic, butter, and vinegar. And roses.

But I can't see. The room's too dark, the pills too small.

The snack in my mouth, my teeth gnawing away, it's a rolled-up, brand-new condom. Lubricated, from the taste of it, the bitter flavor of spermicidal jelly. That slippery feel of K-Y on my tongue.

The wrangler shouts, "Number 72, we need you on set—now. Right now."

Branch Bacardi, everyone, waiting.

So . . . I just point. "That one," I say, still chewing, choking on the bitter taste designed to kill sperm, prevent life, and I just point at a pill. Any pill. It doesn't matter.

146

24

Sheila

Leaning over Ms.
Wright, my fingers pinching a pair of chrome tweezers,
I'm squeezing the sharp points together around a single eyebrow hair. Biting my own tongue. Shutting my
eyes when I yank the hair. Squeezing the tweezers tight
around another stray hair.

Ms. Wright, she doesn't blink. Doesn't flinch or
lean back in her chair to get away. Says how somebody
named Rudolph Valentino, when he died of his appen-
dix, two women in Japan jumped into a live volcano.
This Valentino hoagie-honker, he was a star in silent
pictures, and when he died in 1926 a girl in London
poisoned herself on top a collection of his pictures. An
elevator boy at the Ritz Hotel in Paris poisoned himself on a bed spread with a similar collection. In New
York, two women stood outside the Polyclinic Hospital,
where Valentino died, and cut their wrists. At his funeral, a mob of a hundred thousand rioted and collapsed

the mortuary's front windows, trashing the wreaths and sprays of funeral flowers.

Some wand-waxer named Rudy Vallee recorded a hit song about this Valentino bacon-banger. Called "There's a New Star in Heaven."

True fact.

When her eyebrows look even, I squirt moisturizer onto a little sponge and spread it across her forehead. Dab the sponge across her cheeks and around her eyes.

Our crew of whitewashers, our six hundred sherbet-shooters, they're still home, asleep, with an hour yet to go on their alarm clocks. Today still dark, barely just today. The lighting already set up. Film stock ready. Cameras ready. The Nazi uniforms rented and hanging, still in their dry-cleaner plastic. Nobody here but Ms. Wright and myself.

Her eyes shut, her skin tugged in little directions by the spongeful of moisturizer, Ms. Wright says that morticians style a dead body, apply the makeup, and style the hair from the right side, because that's the side people will see in an open-casket viewing. The funeral director washes the body by hand. Dips cotton balls in insect poison and crams them up your nose to keep bugs from setting up house. Fingers open an anal vent to allow trapped gas to escape. Stuffs plastic cups, like Ping-Pong balls cut in half, under your eyelids to keep them closed. Brushes melted wax on your lips to stop them from peeling.

Me, I'm sponging on foundation. Smoothing a medium-tan shade around her mouth. Blending the edges under her jawline.

Settled in the white makeup chair, the paper bib clipped around her neck, Ms. Wright says how some weed-whacker named Jeff Chandler, he was shooting a movie called *Merrill's Mauraders* in 1961, in the Philippines, and he slipped a disk in his back. This Chandler wiener-wrestler was a big name, a rival to Rock Hudson and Tony Curtis. Recorded a hit album and several singles for Decca. Went under the knife for a quick disk operation. Doctors nicked an artery. Poured fifty-five pints of blood into him, but this Bone-a-Phone still died making that movie.

Her eyes shut, lashes fluttering, brows arched for eye shadow, Ms. Wright says how the Hollywood juice-josher Tyrone Power keeled over dead from a heart attack, filming a sword fight in the film *Solomon and Sheba.*

Ms. Wright says how, when Marilyn Monroe offed herself, Hugh Hefner bought the mausoleum niche next to hers, because he wanted to spend eternity lying next to the most beautiful woman who had ever lived.

Ms. Wright says how the fist-flogger Eric Fleming was shooting on location for his television series *High Jungle* when his canoe overturned in the Amazon River. The current caught Fleming, and the local piranha finished the job. Cameras still rolling.

True fact.

While I'm penciling on her eyeliner, Ms. Wright tells me that page-paster Frank Sinatra got buried with a bottle of Jack Daniel's, a pack of Camel cigarettes, a Zippo lighter, and ten dimes so he could make phone calls. Comic Ernie Kovacs is buried with a pocketful of hand-rolled Havanas.

When fig-fondler Bela Lugosi died in 1956, they buried him in his vampire costume. His funeral could've been one of his own Dracula movies, him wearing those teeth in his coffin. The satin cape, the works.

Walt Disney is not frozen, Ms. Wright says. He's cremated, sealed in a vault with his wife. Greta Garbo's ashes were spread in Sweden. Marlon Brando's were spread around the palm trees of his private South Sea island. In 1988, four years after his death, Peter Lawford still owed ten thousand dollars on his final resting place at the Westwood Village Memorial Park—spitting distance from the most beautiful woman who'd ever lived. So Lawford was evicted, and his ashes were scattered at sea.

By now, I'm brushing on Ms. Wright's blush. Contouring the sides of her nose with dark powder. Tracing the outline of her lips with liner.

The street door swings open to the alley, and a couple members of the crew step inside. Throwing cigarettes behind them. The sound tech and a cameraman, smelling of smoke and cold air. Light in the alley going from black to dark blue. The echoing, far-off ocean rumble of traffic. Morning rush hour.

While I brush on her lip color, Ms. Wright says some wad-dropper named Wallace Reid, the six-foot-one "King of Paramount," died trying to kick morphine in a padded cell.

When sound movies told the world that elegant, ladylike Marie Prevost spoke with a low-class Bronx honk, she quit. Drank herself to death. Died behind her locked apartment door, and her starving dachshund, Maxie, chewed on her for days before the manager bothered to knock.

"Marie Prevost went from the biggest female movie star to dog food—like *that*," says Ms. Wright, and she snaps her fingers.

Movie star Lou Tellegen knelt over a stack of his publicity photos and press clippings and tore out his guts with a pair of scissors. John Bowers walked into the ocean. James Murray jumped into the East River. George Hill blew off his head with a hunting rifle. Milton Sills drove his limousine over Dead Man's Curve on Sunset Boulevard. Beautiful Peg Entwistle climbed the Hollywood sign and leapt to her death. Covergirl Gowili Andre burned to death on a stack of her own magazine photos.

A shot of perfume, a few strokes with a hairbrush, and I'm done.

Ms. Wright opens her eyes.

No poisoned cotton up her nose. No anal vent. Blue contact lenses, the color of desert sky, swim on her eyes. Not Ping-Pong balls cut in half.

Hitler's perfect blond, blue-eyed idea of a sex doll.

Ms. Wright looks at her reflection in the mirror above the dressing table. Twists her neck to see her right profile, left profile. Says, "There are always worse ways to kick the bucket . . ." Her hand plucks a tissue from a box, and her lips say, "I've lived my whole life for myself." With both hands, she pulls the tissue tight and bites her lips together on it. Blotting. Saying, "Not that I'm a patch on Joan Crawford."

Her lips peel off the tissue, leaving a perfect red kiss,

and Ms. Wright says, "But maybe it's time I do something for my kid."

Reaching to take the tissue, I say, "Your little boy?"

And Ms. Wright doesn't say anything. Picks up the tissue kissed with her perfect lips. Hands me the dirty tissue.

25

Mr. 600

Teddy-bear dude
turns sideways to me, twisting his head to the other
side. Dude's thinking I can't see, but from between his
lipsticked lips he pulls a chewed-up, used rubber. Some
old rubber he wore or one he's found on the set, I don't
want to know. After watching my share of faggot porn
flicks, it's no surprise they get off on eating their own
jizz. Eating anybody's.

The kid's showing him both pills, the wood pill and
the cyanide.

The teddy-bear dude points. Dude shrugs his shoulders and points one finger, going, "That one, I guess."

Sheila's holding the door open, lights from the set
blinding us. Sheila goes, "Number 72, if you'd care to
join us . . . please."

The kid hands over that piss-soaked teddy bear. The
kid's fingers are stained black, his skin of his biceps and
lats, his obliques stained blue-black, the color of those le-

sions you get from Kaposi's sarcoma, the gay cancer. The handwriting names of Barbra Streisand and Bo Derek bleeding all over the kid's hand. The kid goes, "Thanks."

On the TVs, it's my whole, entire life passing before my eyes. On one, I'm some presidential dude drilling my tool into the First Lady and Marilyn Monroe until my head gets shot off in some ragtop driving down the street. On another TV, I'm a teenage pizza-delivery dude bringing extra salami to a sorority house.

Kid 72 goes up the stairs, toward Sheila waiting in the doorway. On the top step, he stops and looks back, looking skinny with all the bright lights around him. The kid puts something in his mouth and tosses his head back. Sheila hands him a bottle half full of water, and he takes a swig, bubbles showing every swallow. The door shuts, and he's gone.

The teddy-bear dude's gripping the edge of the buffet table, leaning on it.

I say to him, did his old man ever have any kind of sex talk with him?

The teddy-bear dude goes, "May I borrow your cell phone?"

I go, What for?

And the teddy-bear dude feels around on the table with one hand, picks up a rubber, and puts it into his mouth, spits out the rubber. He goes, "I'd like to call in reinforcements."

Of course I have a phone. In my gym bag. I hand it over, going how in high school I used to date this gal named Brenda, a real fox, a total stone fox, but at the same time a genuine lady.

The teddy-bear dude holds the phone to the top of his

154

nose, leaving just room for one finger to press the buttons. Squinting his eyes, he goes, "I'm listening . . ."

On the TVs, I'm an old geezer pumping a candy-striper in some nursing home. At the same time, another TV shows me as a Cub Scout doing my den mother.

Talking, I go how Brenda was the girl I saw the rest of my life with, us getting married, having babies, Brenda and me building a house and growing old together. Anything, just so long as we were always together. How I felt about her, I loved her too much to ever try and fuck her, so much I didn't even beg to suck her titties or shove my hand down the front of her jeans. We had that kind of mutual affection and respect.

On the phone, the teddy-bear dude says, "Lenny?" Still gripping the table with his other hand, the dude goes, "I need to place a rush order."

Sophomore year, I loved Brenda so much I showed her picture to my old man.

Here's how he always was: My old man took the snapshot from my fingers. He looked at it, shaking his head. He handed Brenda back to me, saying, "How's a doofus like you rate something so fine?" My old man goes, "Kid, that snatch is way, way out of your league."

And I go how I wanted to marry her.

On the TVs I'm a soldier, a grunt private dodging Jap bombs and banging Hawaiian babes in Hawaii in *From Her to Eternity*.

On the phone, the teddy-bear dude says, "Right now, I need an escort, anybody with a dick, any race or age, so long as he can get hard, pump, dump, and bail." Teddy-bear dude says, "No, he's not for me." Dude goes, "I'm never that desperate."

155

When I said my plan to marry Brenda, my old man smiled. He smiled and threw his arm across my shoulders. He goes, "You dork her yet?"

I shake my head no.

And my old man goes, "You want a surefire way to not get a gal knocked up?"

The teddy-bear dude catches me looking at him, and the dude goes, "Keep talking, I swear I'm listening . . ."

My old man said the way ancient dudes never got their ladies pregnant, before rubbers and birth-control pills and sponges and shit, was, a little bit after they shot their wad, with their dick still buried deep, ancient dudes knew to piss just a dribble. Just let a trickle of piss leak out. Piss, my old man said, was enough acid to kill the sperm.

He means to pee inside her.

He says Brenda won't know.

My old man says this trick is something all caring dads tell their sons. It's a kind of legacy they hand down from generation to generation, and if I ever have a little boy, I'll tell him the same.

That sophomore year was the last great time in my life. I had a girl I loved. I had a dad who loved me.

On the phone, the teddy-bear dude says, "Fifty bucks, take it or leave it." Dude laughs and says, "You must have some loser, a meth head or junkie, who'll stop by for fifty bucks . . ."

My night I finally made love to Brenda, it was beautiful. We spread a blanket under a tree covered with little pink flowers, just stars and flowers above us. We brought a bottle of wine my old man gave me for the occasion. Champagne. Brenda baked chocolate-chip cookies, and we got a little loaded and made love. Not like in movies, where it's a dick and pussy in a battle to the death, porking and banging and slamming, but more like our skin was having a conversation. By smells and tastes and touch, we were finding out about each other. Saying what we couldn't with words.

Both of us naked on the blanket, little flower petals falling on us, Brenda asked if I brought some protection.

And I put my finger touching her lips and told her not to worry. I said my dad told me the secret to being careful.

On the phone, the teddy-bear dude says, "I don't care how scuzzy and old the guy looks. Even if he's fat and disgusting, I'll pay the fifty bucks."

Under that tree of little flowers, Brenda and me held on to each other, carried each other through our first climax together, the start of our lifetime. The promise ring was around her finger, and we'd drunk the bottle of wine. We stayed wrapped together, me on top of her, still inside, and aching to take a leak from all that sweet champagne.

On the TV screens, I'm a gray-haired millionaire tycoon giving it to my secretary across a carved wood desk. Other screens, I'm a plumber snaking the pipes of a bored housewife.

Laying inside Brenda, just so to protect her, I let a little piss leak out. That bladder of mine was busting, and my flow couldn't shut off. My little dribble kept

157

gushing, and Brenda rolled her eyes to look into my eyes, our eyes close to touching, our noses touching, her lips brushing my lips.

Brenda said, "What are you doing?"

And bearing down to stop, clamping down to not piss, still inside her, I said, "Nothing." I go, "I'm not doing anything."

On the phone, the teddy-bear dude goes, "You have somebody in mind?" He laughs and says, "I told you, I don't care how gross . . ."

Brenda wrestled against me, rolling side to side on the blanket and beating me with her fists. She kept saying, "You pig. You're a pig." Underneath my hips, Brenda bucked and squirmed, telling me to get off her. To pull out.

And I kept saying, not yet. My hands holding her arms, I kept saying this was to keep her safe.

On the TVs, I'm in ancient times, doggy-styling Cleopatra. I'm an astronaut, doing round-the-world with a green alien babe in a zero-gravity space station.

Under those flowers and stars, on top of Brenda, I couldn't stop until she worked one knee up between my legs, kicked her knee up, fast, and crushed my balls. With that smack, the pain took over. My dick twisted out, popped out, still rock-hard, piss still spraying, hot champagne piss hosing all over both of us. I grabbed my crushed nuts in both hands, letting go of Brenda's arms, and she rolled out from under me.

Something fell and hit the side of my face, too hard to be a little flower, hurting too bad to be spit. Brenda grabbed her empty clothes and took off running, and that's the last and final time I saw her: running away from behind, with my piss running down the insides of both her thighs.

The teddy-bear dude goes, "Fine, send whoever, just send him now." Dude shuts the phone and hands it over to me.

That's how come I advised the kid the way I did.

Teddy-bear dude makes a face, spits something chewed-up on the floor. Another condom. He squints his eyes at me and says, "You suggested that confused young man urinate inside of his mother?"

No, I go. And explain about the cyanide pill Cassie wanted, how I was supposed to bring it inside the locket, but the kid agreed to carry the pill to her.

And the teddy-bear dude, his mouth falls open fast as his eyebrows jump up. His face comes back together, the dude swallows and goes, "Those two pills he showed me—you're saying one was cyanide?"

And I nod my head yeah.

Both of us, we're looking at the closed door to the set.

On the TVs, I'm an old-time caveman daisy-chained in an orgy with a tribe of other humanoids, dirty and hairy and hunched over, none of us quite human, not yet evolved.

The teddy-bear dude shrugs his shoulders, going, "Even if the kid takes the wrong pill, we'll still set the world record." Dude says, "I called an agency, and the cavalry is on its way."

Dude says how this agency knows somebody who'll do an hour for less than fifty bucks. Some old dude, the agency says, the joke of the adult industry, flabby and wrinkled, with scabby, peeling skin. Bloodshot eyes

159

and bad breath. Some porn dinosaur the agency can't book, they said they'd try and contact him, rush him over here so he can fill in for kid 72. In case the kid's dead or gone limp or told Cassie he loves her and gets kicked out.

Teddy-bear dude goes, "Based on their description, I can't wait to see how bad this monster might look." He's blinking his eyes, looking out one eye, then the other. He rubs his eyes with the heels of both hands, blinks fast, and squints up at the TV screens, frowning.

On the TVs, I'm a totally buff naked model in the center of a figure-drawing class, getting sucked off by beautiful coed art students.

What bounced off my skull that night, my last night with Brenda, what hit me too hard to be a little pink flower—it was my promise ring I'd gave her.

In my hand, my phone starts to ring. From the number on the screen, the incoming call is my booking agent.

26

Mr. 72

The stopwatch girl

lets me come back, on account of I have to give Mr. Bacardi something important. She leads me back down the stairs, to the waiting basement. The smell of baby oil and cheese crackers.

The minute Mr. Bacardi sees me, he presses his cell phone to his chest and says, "You kill her?"

The Dan Banyan guy says, "Or, worse . . . did you say you *loved* her?"

And the stopwatch girl says, "Gentlemen, may I have your attention . . ."

When a guy goes up there to be with Cassie Wright, he might as well be visiting her in the hospital. They got her laid in a white bed with white sheets and pillows, laying with her legs open, sipping orange juice from a glass through a plastic bendy straw. Her bottom half covered with a sheet. The lights shine on the bed, hot and bright as an operating room. And when the girl

161

with the clipboard brings you in, Cassie Wright might as well be a lady in bed waiting for some nurse to clean up her just-born baby so Cassie can feed it.

Crowded around the head of the bed, they got flowers in vases and wrapped in bouquets, roses and roses and roses. Every different kind, but all roses. And standing up, on the tables beside her pillows, they crowded greetings cards, frilly with lacy edges and sparkling with glitter. Cards tucked in bouquets. Cards knocked on the floor and printed with the dirty tread of somebody's shoe stepped on them.

All those cards, Mother's Day cards. "To the World's Best Mom!" And "To the Best Mother a Boy Could Ever Have!"

The stopwatch girl brings you in, tugging by one arm, and she says, "Ms. Wright . . ." The girl points at the flowers I'm holding and says, "We've brought you another son . . ."

In the waiting basement, afterward, the Dan Banyan guy says, "Your mother is such a hoot!" He says, "You think, if I asked, would she go out to dinner with me?"

Yelling into his cell phone, Mr. Bacardi says, "How can you say that?" He yells, "I have the deepest, most even, darkest, best tan in the industry!"

Crowding the room for the movie set, folks with their clothes on, they were balancing cameras on one shoulder, or holding and watching the slack cords that snaked from each camera to plug into some power boxes, to wall outlets, to other cords. Other folks waved sticks with a microphone dangled from one end. Folks leaned over Cassie Wright with lipsticks and combs.

162

They monkeyed with the bright lights and tinkered with shiny silver umbrellas that bounced the light to land on Cassie in her bed.

The whole family of them, laughing, their eyes bloodshot from staying up all hours, waiting for a baby to be born. People with pretty Mother's Day cards stuck to the underneath of their shoes, tracked around the little room. Rose petals were scattered everywhere.

The stopwatch girl steers you in through the door, pinching you by the elbow, and a guy holding a camera says, "Crimony, Cass, how many kids did you have?"

Folks laugh, everybody but me.

That whole family you're being born into.

Talking around a lipstick stuck in her mouth, sunk in her bed, Cassie Wright says, "Today, I've had them all."

Back in the basement, Mr. Bacardi tells his cell phone, "My best work is *not* behind me!" He yells, "You know, nobody does a better split-reed standing anal with an on-demand hands-free pop-shot release."

And the Dan Banyan guy looks up at the TV screens and says, "You think she'd marry me?"

Kicked against one wall of the set, the three Nazi uniforms sat in a pile, dark with sweat. The stopwatch girl said the crew stopped using them halfway through, to go faster.

A guy held the glass of juice close enough Cassie Wright could make her lips go around the straw. As she sucked some orange juice, the guy looked at me and said, "Come on, kid. Climb on top." He said, "Some of us want to go home tonight."

Cassie Wright pushed him away with one hand.

With her other hand, she waved me closer, she scooped that hand under her breast, and stretched the nipple toward me, saying, "Don't take his shit. He's just the director." Cassie held out her breast, saying, "Come to Momma . . ."

Her left breast, the better of the two. Same as I had at home. Used to have. At the house where I used to live, before my adopted folks changed the locks.

Mr. Bacardi on his cell phone says, "Twenty bucks? To drop by and dip my wick for thirty seconds?" He looks over at the Dan Banyan guy and says, "Are you sure you don't mean fifty bucks?"

Still squinting at the monitors, the Dan Banyan guy says, "The queen of porn and the king of prime-time television, getting married." He says, "We could have our own reality show."

On the television he's watching, it's not even Cassie Wright. The movie's showing some in-between shot of a bulldozer dumping dirt into a dump truck.

On the set, one step closer, rose petals stuck to my bare feet, I knelt down next to her big bright bed.

The only folks watching looked at us through the camera or faced the other way, watching us on a video screen, hearing us talk through wires inside their head-phones.

And me kneeling next to the bed, Cassie Wright scooping one breast into my face, I asked, did she recognize me?

"Suck," she said, and rubbed her nipple across my lips.

I asked, did she know who I was?

And Cassie Wright smiled, saying, "Are you the one bags my groceries at the supermarket?"

Blinking and squinting at the TVs, the Dan Banyan guy says, "We'll get hitched in Las Vegas. It will be the media event of the decade."

Yelling at his cell phone, Mr. Bacardi says, "My fans don't want any new face. My fans want me!"

I'm her son, I said to Cassie Wright. The baby she gave up for adoption.

"Told you so," said the guy holding the juice.

I've come here because she wouldn't answer my letters.

"Not another one . . ." said the guy balancing the camera, his voice buried behind the metal and plastic of it, his lens so close in my face I could see myself talking, reflected in curved glass.

Recorded. Being filmed. Watched by people, forever.

When I opened my lips to speak, Cassie stuffed her nipple in my mouth. To talk, I had to twist my head away, saying, "No." The taste of salt on her breast skin, the flavor of other men's spit. I said, "I'm here to give you a new life."

And the stopwatch girl lifted the clock from around her neck and with her thumb pressed the button on top. She said, "Go."

How I feel is how the sex surrogate looked with all her air leaked out. Flat. Crumpled. Before my adopted mom shook the pink skin in the face of my adopted dad and both of them shook her in the face of Minister Harner, turning my secret, most favorite love into

165

what I hated most in the world. Not my adopted dad's tiny, hand-detailed crack whores, or my adopted mom's cherry-vanilla-frosted pussies, it's my pink shadow showed to everybody.

The only thing that made me special, now my worst shame.

To prove I'm me, I showed Cassie the gold heart Branch Bacardi wore. Undoing the chain from around my wrist, I pried open the heart and showed her the baby picture of me inside. The cyanide pill, I dumped into one hand and made a fist around.

Cassie Wright's smiling face—looking at the baby picture, her face got old around her eyes and mouth. Her lips went thin, and the skin on her cheeks sagged to bunch against her neck. She said, "Where'd you get this?"

Irving, I told her.

And Cassie Wright said, "You mean Irwin?"

I nodded yes.

She said, "Did he give you anything else?"

My fingers fisted tighter around the pill, and I shook my head no.

That's me, the baby inside the heart, I told her. I'm her son.

And Cassie Wright smiled again, saying, "Don't take this too hard, kid," she said, "but the baby I gave up for adoption wasn't a little boy." She snapped her heart shut, taking the locket and chain. Cassie lifted both arms until her hands met at the back of her neck. Clipping the chain, she said, "I told people it was a boy, but she was a beautiful little girl . . ."

The stopwatch click-click-clicking to make minutes.

166

The camera lens reflected me so close up all I could see was one big tear roll down from my eye.

"Now," Cassie Wright said. She pulled the bedsheet off her bottom half and said, "Be a good boy, and start fucking me."

In the basement waiting place, the Dan Banyan guy says, "So what did you do with the cyanide pill?"

I don't know.

I put it in the crotch of my shorts. First wadded on the floor. Later, for safekeeping, held under my balls.

And the Dan Banyan guy makes a face, saying, "How can you expect anyone to put that in their mouth after it's been in your dirty shorts?"

"It's cyanide!" yells Mr. Bacardi, holding his phone to his chest. He says, "A little sweat and smegma is not going to make it any more poisoner."

Punch-fucking Cassie Wright, hard, one leg bent back so far her knee's in her face, I heard the stopwatch girl say, "Time."

Still fucking her, rolled over and nailing her on her side, her legs jackknifed, I heard Cassie Wright say, "This kid fucks like he's got something to prove."

Stuffing her doggy style, on all fours, my hands grabbed full of her wet, loose ass-skin, I heard Cassie Wright say, "Get this little bastard off of me!"

Hands came around me from behind. Fingers dug my fingers out of her thighs. Folks were pulling me back until only my dick was still touching her, my hips still bucking until just the head of my dick was inside her, until I popped free, my 'nads jumping out ribbon after ribbon of white ooze across her butt.

At the far end of her, Cassie Wright's mouth said, "You guys getting this?"

The director said, "This is one for the trailer." He sipped orange juice from the cup's bendy straw and said, "Careful, kid, you're fixing to drown us."

Cassie Wright said, "Somebody wipe me off." Still on her hands and knees, she looked back over one shoulder, saying, "Good to meet you, kid. Keep buying my movies, okay?"

In the basement, a voice says, "Number 600?" A girl's voice. The stopwatch girl says, "We're ready for you on the set, please."

Into his cell phone, Mr. Bacardi yells, "I made your lousy agency." He yells, "It's not the money, it's the disrespect!" But he starts toward the stairway, the stopwatch girl, the set.

Before Mr. Bacardi can head up the stairs, I reach into my shorts, feeling between the tight elastic crotch and the baggy folds of my ball skin. I say to wait. And, fingering my nuts, I jump the one, two, three steps up to where Mr. Bacardi stands.

I say to kill her. Kill the Wright bitch. To murder her.

"You can't *kill* her," says the Dan Banyan guy. "I'm going to *marry* her."

Mr. Bacardi folds his phone shut, still saying, "Twenty lousy bucks . . ."

Just how he planned, I say to fuck her to death. And I drop the pill into his hand.

27

Mr. 137

Wouldn't you know
it? I'm not even married to Cassie Wright and already
I'm about to become a widower. To the young actor 72,
I say, Please. Please tell me that was merely an M&M
candy he gave Bacardi.

"Potassium cyanide," says the talent wrangler as she
leans over to pick up a paper napkin off the floor. "Found
naturally in the cassava or manioc roots native to Africa,
used to tint architectural blueprints in the form of the
deep-blue pigment known as Prussian blue. Hence the
shade 'cyan' blue . . ."

Hence, she says, the term "cyanosis," used to describe the blue tinge of someone's skin after she's been
poisoned with cyanide. Instant and certain and forever,
death.

On the monitors hanging above the room, echoing
and empty save for the three of us, a full-breasted Cassie
Wright plays a stern ward nurse, righteous and tyran-

nical in her starched white uniform and sensible shoes, who brings joy and freedom to the residents of a men's mental hospital by giving them all blow jobs. A classic of adult culture called *One Flew over the Cuckoo's Nuts*.

I say how much I love this movie.

And the young actor 72 says, "What are you talking about?"

He says the film we're watching is about a feisty young pitcher who earns herself a starting spot on an all-male softball team by giving her teammates blow jobs.

Squinting, standing on my tiptoes and peering to see the screen above us, one of my hands still clamps on the edge of a folding buffet table. My anchor. A landmark in the dark room.

Actor 72 says, "This movie's called *The Bad Juiced Bears*." He says, "Are you blind?"

It doesn't matter if Bacardi gives Cassie the pill or not, the wrangler says, stacking paper cups and stuffing them with crumpled napkins. She says the production might already have its dead body. A dead man, walking. Some man about to collapse at any minute. Cyanide, she says, travels as ions through the bloodstream, binding to the iron atom of the enzyme cytochrome c oxidase in the mitochondria of muscle cells. This union changes the shape of the cell, denaturing it to the effect the cell is no longer able to absorb oxygen. Effected cells, primarily the central nervous system and the heart, can no longer produce energy.

For my reality show, after Cassie and I are married, I ask, How about calling it *Sex Pot and the Private Dick*?

Gathering empty potato-chip bags, balling them up, and stuffing them into a black garbage bag, the talent wrangler says, "Most cyanide poisoning occurs trans-dermally." Looking at actor 72, she says, "How do you feel?"

Any weakness? Any loss of hearing? Weakness in his hands? Sweating, dizziness, or anxiety?

Cyanide is what killed those nine hundred people in the Jonestown mass suicide of 1978. Cyanide killed the millions in Nazi concentration camps. It killed Hitler and his wife, Eva Braun. During the Cold War of the 1950s, American spies were issued eyeglasses with thick, clunky frames. If captured, they were trained to casually chew the curved earpieces, where fatal doses of cyanide were cast inside the plastic. It's these same horn-rimmed suicide glasses, the wrangler says, that inspired the look of Buddy Holly and Elvis Costello. All those young hipsters wearing death on their nose.

The moment the wrangler says "Jonestown" the actor and I look at the punch bowl, half empty, cigarette butts and orange peels floating in the pink lemonade.

About my new reality show with Cassie, I ask what if we call it *Under-Cover Coupling*. I ask does that sound too racy for network television.

And actor 72 says, "What's trans . . ."

"Transdermal," the talent wrangler says. "It means 'through the skin.' "

Wiping up crumbs with the edge of her hand, clearing the buffet tables, the wrangler says how most cyanide poisoning happens through people's skin. To the young actor, she says, "Smell your hand."

The kid cups one hand over his nose and sniffs.

"No," the wrangler says, "smell the hand in which you held the pill."

The actor sniffs his other hand, sniffs again, and says, "Almonds?"

That smell of bitter almonds is the potassium cyanide of the pill reacting with the dampness of his hand to form hydrogen cyanide. Already, the poison's leaching into his bloodstream.

"I'll just wash my hands," the actor says.

And the wrangler shakes her head, saying that's not the only place the pill touched. Not the only sweaty spot on his body dense with pores and nerve endings.

About my future reality show with my future, maybe dead wife, I ask why don't we call it *Mrs. Curves and the Flat Foot*.

Actor 72 looks from the wrangler, tucking his chin to his chest to look straight down at his crotch, saying, "No way."

The wrangler blots a puddle of spilled soda, using a handful of napkins.

The wrangler picks up unopened condoms, red, pink, and blue condoms, and drops them into an empty popcorn bag.

Actor 72 sniffs his hand again, then leans over. With his other hand he stretches out the waistband of his briefs. Bending over, his spine a curve of knobs under his skin, the actor inhales a long breath through his nose. He bends over again and takes another long, long sniff. Standing straight, he says, "I can't get close enough."

To me, he says, "Do me a favor?" He says, "Sniff my nuts?"

The talent wrangler is grabbing up handfuls of spilled

172

candy—jawbreakers and candy corn and gum balls rolling around loose on the buffet tables.

"Please," actor 72 says to me, "my life depends on it."

Wouldn't you know it? This would happen only after I found out I was heterosexual.

If the young man ate candy, the wrangler says, that's probably what's kept him alive so long. Glucose is a natural antidote to cyanide poisoning. Based on anecdotal evidence, glucose binds with the cyanide to produce less toxic compounds.

Actor 72 sprints to the buffet table and stands next to my hand where it's clamped on the table's edge. There his fingers scramble to collect the leftover Lemonheads and Skittles, the fun-sized Butterfingers and Hershey Kisses, and cram them into his mouth. Chewing Red Vines licorice and jelly beans, his mouth gummy and sloshing with spit and sugar, the actor turns to me, saying, "Please." Around wads of thin mints and chocolate turtles, he says, "Just smell me, okay?"

The mad monk Grigory Rasputin, who seduced and manipulated the women of the Russian court with his reported eighteen-inch penis, the wrangler says the corrupt monk survived several plots to kill him with cyanide because each assassin mixed the poison in something sweet: sugary wine or candy or pastries. Mixing the toxins with their most effective counteragent.

At this moment, the wrangler says, Branch Bacardi would merely need to insert the pill inside Cassie Wright. Whether it was swallowed or otherwise, Cassie would suffer giddiness, confusion, headaches. Cassie's skin would turn a faint blue, and her heart would race as it tried to feed her cells more oxygen they couldn't absorb. She'd lapse into a coma, suffer a heart attack, and be dead within a few words' time.

"Even if you do sniff his nuts," the wrangler says to me, "not every human being can detect the smell of hydrogen cyanide."

From outside, somewhere above and beyond this place, comes the wail of sirens, getting louder, sirens getting closer.

The talent wrangler reaches across the table, picking up half-eaten cupcakes. Pizza crusts. Soggy maple bars licked clean of their frosting.

The sirens arrive here, wailing just beyond the concrete walls.

"If you intend to approach Ms. Wright," the wrangler says, speaking to me, "don't imagine you can just waltz into her life."

She stoops to pinch something off the floor. Frowning at it, held between two fingers, she says, "Some crazy person chewed up the condoms . . . ?"

And I shrug and say, It takes all kinds.

Scraping up a wad of gum, using the toe of her shoe, she tells me how it took her months of trying to meet Cassie. How Cassie mentioned a child she'd given up for adoption, how that was the biggest mistake of her life, something Cassie could never repair. It wasn't too much effort to guilt Cassie into making this movie, to leave that lost child a fortune. To wrap up and clean up the mess of Cassie Wright's sad, wasted life.

The sirens so close by now, so loud, the wrangler has to shout.

Still wiping up crumbs, scrubbing sticky strands of

174

candy off the tables, the wrangler shouts, "It's only hate makes you that patient."

She shouts that nothing except a lifetime of festering anger and hatred would give you the determination to wait around corners for hours, rain or shine, to loiter at bus stops just in case Cassie Wright happened by. To get revenge.

The sirens cut off, leaving us in silence, the wrangler, actor 72, and I looking at each other in the empty room.

And, whispering, but still loud in the new quiet, actor 72 says, "You're her."

The actor 72 swallows his mess of sugar and spit and says, "You're Cassie Wright's lost baby." Saying, "And Cassie doesn't even know."

Crushing an empty aluminum can in one fist, the wrangler says, "Correction . . ." Smiling. She says, "As of this minute, I am that *very wealthy* lost little baby."

The talent wrangler—her nose is Branch Bacardi's long, straight nose. Her black hair is his. Her lips are his lips.

I ask how come she knows so much about cyanide.

And wouldn't you know it, actor 72 sprints to the bathroom to scrub his balls.

175

28

Sheila

Maybe one cigarette before I bring in Branch Bacardi, our anchorman, Ms. Wright points a fingernail at her cup of orange juice. Hooks her finger for me to bring her the cup. Waves one, two, three quick waves for me to bring her over the juice, fast.

The cup with the straw, I bring it. Bend the straw to the level of her mouth.

Ms. Wright curls a finger for me to lean in closer. Near enough I can smell her sweat. See the gray roots of her blond hair. In one breath, smell the low-tide stink of old semen. In another breath, the dusty powder smell of condom latex. The bright smell of orange juice. Her lips, ignoring the straw, they say, "I know." They whisper, "I've known since we met at the coffee shop." Soft as a lullaby, Ms. Wright says, "I almost cried, you look so much like me . . ."

True fact.

Twisting her head sideways, dodging the drinking straw, Ms. Wright smiles her lipstick at me and says, "To quote that last young man . . . I wanted to give you a new life."

She says how Richard Burton was almost killed while filming *Night of the Iguana* with Ava Gardner in Mexico. At the height of the third act, Burton was supposed to cut the rope that trapped a live iguana and let it escape into the jungle. Of course he cut, but the trouble was the iguana had spent weeks and weeks with hard-boozing Ava, Richard, and John Huston. The lizard didn't run anywhere. To make the scene work, the crew wired the iguana, and the moment Burton set it free, they hit the lizard with 110 volts.

Trouble was, Richard Burton was still touching the iguana. He took the whole charge, through the lizard, and was almost electrocuted. The world's most famous actor and a creepy, scaly, cold-blooded reptile almost fried to death by the same surge of electric current.

True fact.

At this, Ms. Wright smiled and said, "Enjoy spending all that life insurance money . . ."

And before she could say another word, I shoved the plastic drinking straw into her mouth. Stuffed it all the way to the back of her throat. Gagged the witch into silence.

29

Mr. 72

The stopwatch girl
steps her feet left, then right, then left down the stairs,
the fingers of both hands cupped over her mouth. Over-
lapping each other, tight, like to keep something inside
her mouth. Her eyes go big around and forget to blink,
so dry they don't shine except the little bit that glass
might shine. The glass in her hanging stopwatch. Her
fingers pressed until the skin's gone white, any blood
pressed out of the skin of her fingers and face as she
steps down, left then right, each foot lower.

I don't know.

Anytime you need to watch somebody die, die for
real, check out how they get their orgasm at the end of
a porn. Their mouth biting to get just one more inhale
of air. Their neck roped with veins and strings of muscle
to make the skin webbed, and their chin working, their
teeth reaching out and digging the air. All the skin
of their cheeks pulling their lips back, stretching their

ears back, skin crushing their eyes shut, as their front teeth try to bite off the biggest next chunk of life.

Watch *World Whore Three* and you'll see how certain folks say the death scene is just another cum shot.

The stopwatch girl steps down to the basement floor and stands there. She rips the pink skin off her hands, then a blue layer of skin—rubber gloves, pulled inside out—and throws them on the floor, where they spread, flat and dead as a sex surrogate. The girl's bare hands slide up to cover her whole face. Her hand skin old with wrinkles and pickled from stewing inside those gloves. Her shoulders rise, her curved backbone straightens as she breathes in one big inhale of the piss smell, the baby oil and sweat of here. The breath holds inside her, her elbows crushed on top of her boobs, her elbows touching together. The breath sighs out in broken mouthfuls, jerking her whole body.

Watching her, my balls are scrubbed red. My shorts, soaked wet from the sink. I'm homeless. An orphan. Broke and unemployed.

The Dan Banyan guy, he's looking. Not straight at the girl, but turning his ear to where she's crying, really crying now, her breath muffled behind her fingers, her face burrowing into her open hands. The 137 guy says, "Is Cassie dead?"

Cold and broke, orphaned and rubbed raw, I peel my feet the left, right, left, right sticky steps over to stand next to the girl. In just only my wet underpants, I put an arm around her shoulders, the knots of her sweater shaking. I wrap my other arm around her until she's wearing me. Until the stopwatch girl stops shaking. My chin hooked over her shoulder, holding her head

179

tight against my chest, I look down to see the writing on my arm.

Petting her hair with one hand, I tell her, "My name's not really number 72 . . ."

I don't know.

Dead flakes of her head, sticking to my hand, showering to the floor. The stopwatch girl coming apart. I sniff my fingers and say I like the smell of her shampoo. I say at least she knows her real birth mom. The cold feel of her stopwatch pushed into my bellybutton. Holding her until she's just breathing regular, I ask what's her name.

And the girl pulls back a little. The silver crucifix hanging around my neck, it's stuck to her cheek, and hangs there, pressed into her skin. She pulls back, and the gold chain of the crucifix loops between us, connecting her and me. Another breath and the crucifix peels off, falls back to my chest, leaving a red shape of it dented into her face.

Her stopwatch has stamped a round clock shape around my bellybutton.

The girl says, still in my arms, she says, "This is how much my mother hated me . . ." She says, "I tell people my name is Sheila because my real mother gave me the ugliest name she could imagine."

The name on her birth certificate, from when Cassie Wright gave her away.

With the gun finger of one hand, the girl flicks the tears off each cheek, fast as windshield wipers, and she says, "The bitch named me Zelda Zonk." She smiles and says, "How's that for hatred?"

Holding her, it's not so important how I have nothing outside of this moment, outside of this place. How I have no idea of my real name or who I am. How, right here, her sweater against my skin, this moment feels like enough.

And the Dan Banyan guy says, "Did you say 'Zelda Zonk'?" Across the basement, smiling, looking at us with his ear, guy 137 says, "Did she really name you Zelda Zonk?" And, shaking his head, he starts to laugh.

And I say my real name is Darin, Darin Johnson, holding Zelda until her cheek comes back to rest against the cross on my chest. Her stopwatch clock tick-tick-ticking against the skin of my gut.

30

Mr. 137

The head of casting
for Metro-Goldwyn-Mayer rejected Roy Fitzgerald
three times. The actor stumbled when asked to walk
around her office, stumbled so often she worried he'd
break her glass coffee table. Fitzgerald, a former navy
sailor turned Teamster, who now worked delivering
frozen carrots, showed too much gum line when he
smiled. Worst of all, he giggled. Fitzgerald spoke with
the squeal of a teenage girl, and every time he tripped
and stumbled over his own feet he'd giggle.

Nobody would cast the big sissy until his agent,
Henry Willson, taught him to press his lips to his teeth
as he smiled. Willson exposed Fitzgerald to an actor suf-
fering from strep throat. Once Fitzgerald was infected
and his throat fully inflamed, the agent ordered him
to scream and shout until his vocal cords were scarred.
After that, the actor's voice was lower, a deep, gravelly

growl. A man's voice. And his name was changed to Rock Hudson.

I love that Cassie Wright knew that bit of Hollywood history. The fact that we both knew so much of the same trivia—about Tallulah drinking crushed eggshells and Lucy stretching her face back—that made me fall in love with her. Most marriages are based on a lot less.

Cassie knew about Marilyn Monroe cutting one high heel shorter than the other so her ass would truly roll as she walked. Cassie knew that Marilyn's lifetime of pneumonia and bronchitis was most likely caused by her habit of burying herself in a bathtub of crushed ice before any appearance in film or public. Lying naked, drugged to escape the pain, buried in ice for hours, gave Monroe the solid stand-up tits and ass she wanted for the day's work.

Wouldn't you know it?

Cassie knew Marilyn's secret name, the person Monroe dreamed of being. Not the baby-talking, hip-swinging blonde. Monroe dreamed of being respected, an intellectual like Arthur Miller, a respected, Stanislavsky-trained actor. A dignified human being. That's who Monroe would become as she traveled without makeup, without designer clothes borrowed from a movie studio, with her famous hair tied under a scarf, hiding behind horn-rimmed reading glasses. It was that plain, intelligent, educated actress who called herself Zelda Zonk. When she booked airplane tickets or registered in hotels. Zelda Zonk. Who read books. Who collected art. That was who Marilyn Monroe, the blonde sex goddess, dreamed of being.

31

Sheila

Ms. Wright knew.

All along, the woman knew who I was. Who she
really was. She played along, knowing she would die.
Cassie Wright would willingly fuck six hundred pud-
pullers to make me rich.

True fact. Another last thing today comes down to
is reality.

What do you do when your entire identity is destroyed in an instant? How do you cope when your
whole life story turns out to be wrong?

That *bitch*.

32

Mr. 600

On the TVs, they're
playing the first movie Cassie ever appeared in. Shot on
video, maybe one step better than some security camera
at the corner quick-stop grocery. On the TVs is her and
me, young as Sheila and the kid 72. Cassie's eyes are
rolled up to show only white, her arms flopping loose
at her sides, her head rolling around on her neck so far
the pull opens her mouth, drool sliding out the corner
of her lips.

Slack as a blow-up sex-doll version of herself.

If you want to know, that first film I did with Cassie
Wright, I slipped her a diet soda mixed with beta-
ketamine and Demerol. With the camera set up on a
tripod next to the mattress, I fucked her everywhere my
dick would fit.

Because I loved her so much.

That first movie was called *Frisky Business*. After she

185

got famous, the distributor recut it and released the movie as *Lay Misty for Me*. Recut as *World Whore One*.

If you got to know, Cassie never planned to make that first movie.

That movie's playing to the empty basement.

The kid's in the john, scrubbing any poison off his gonads, scrubbing the way the teddy-bear dude scrubbed his forehead.

Sheila comes down the stairs, blubbering. Dragging her sleeves of her sweater across her eyes, smearing snot and whatnot sideways to her ears, her top teeth meeting her bottom teeth on edge, and her jaw bunched with muscle at the corners. She's saying, "Fucker . . ." Sheila wings the clipboard across the room, where it hits the wall to explode in paper names and numbers. A fluttering cloud of fifty- and twenty-dollar bills that Sheila took as bribe money.

The kid comes out the bathroom door saying, "Don't cry." Saying, "It's what Miss Wright wanted . . ."

Just graduated from Missoula High School, Cassie had this big plan to go to drama school. She planned to live at home and study to be an actor or a movie star—either way, so long as she was in show business. Either way, she didn't want to marry me. How she told me was her grades were too good. Cassie said maybe if she was stupid and desperate, really clutching at straws and emotionally needy, utterly destroyed, she'd accept my proposal—so I figured there was still hope.

Trouble was, her folks had poisoned her against me with all this self-esteem crap.

The Friday night Cassie told me, I said I understood.

186

I said I wanted her to live the full, rich life's dream she cherished. And I asked, did she want a diet soda?

The closest thing that comes to how today felt is when you wipe back to front. You're on the toilet. You're not thinking, and you smear shit on the back of your hanging-down wrinkled ball skin. The more you try to wipe it clean, the skin stretches, and the mess keeps getting bigger. The thin layer of shit spreads into the hair and down your thighs. That's how a day like this, how it felt.

Later, Cassie told me the drugs, the beta-ketamine and Demerol, stopped her heart. Her brain cooled, and she rose up out of her body, hovering near the ceiling, looking down, her and the video camera watching my ass clench and relax, clench and relax, as I fucked her until her heart started back to pump. Fucked her to death, then back to life. Humping her dead body around that mattress, I ended the old life she had, wanting to act, and gave her a new life.

Sex reincarnated that good, pure girl, but as something else.

Cassie hovering, watching the action same as I'm doing now.

Behind Sheila, the teddy-bear dude comes down the stairs into the basement. Both his hands clutching the rail at one side.

Sheila yanks the stopwatch, snapping the cord around her neck, and pitches the watch against the concrete wall. Another little explosion.

Another step down, and Sheila says, "The pig took the pill himself."

The kid crosses to his brown paper bag, pulls out tennis shoes, jeans, a T-shirt. A belt. Stepping into his socks, he says, "Who?"

Sheila folds her arms. Looking up at a TV, at me humping Cassie Wright's limp body, she says, "My father."

The teddy-bear dude says, "Who?"

Branch Bacardi.

Me. Dead and hovering, the way Cassie floated up after her heart stopped.

Six hundred dudes. One gal. A world record for the ages. A must-have movie for every discerning collector of things erotic.

Didn't one of us on purpose set out to make a snuff movie. That's a lie.

If you imagined I was alive, that's another. I took the pill.

Buttoning his shirt, the kid says, "Is Mr. Bacardi dead?"

And Sheila says it's hard to tell. She says, "With his tan, and all the bronzer he has on, he looks healthier and more alive than any of us."

My daughter.

On the TVs, I'm popping my load deep inside Cassie's dead snatch, pumping her back to life. A decent money shot wasted, worthless for nothing except making some kid. Sheila. Stupid, stupid me.

33

Mr. 72

We're afterward now.

We're standing in the alley, after the paramedics asked Sheila was there any next-of-kin? Any family to be notified?

This is after Sheila shook her head no. White flakes drifting off her hair, small as ashes from a fire, and she told them, "Nobody. The pig had no one."

Mr. Bacardi had nobody.

It's after we left the Dan Banyan guy in the basement, him getting dressed but wearing his shirt inside out. Feeling the buttons, he said, "For our reality show, how about calling it *The Blonde Leading the Blind?*" He pulled his pants on backward, then rightward. Then, fishing a phone out of his pants pocket, Dan Banyan punched speed-dial, and when somebody answered he says not to send the escort. Everything's over. The old, flabby guy they were sending, he's not needed.

The job is done.

After the Dan Banyan guy calls someone else to say yes, yes, yes to some emergency hair transplants. After he calls a restaurant to reserve a table for him and Miss Wright, for tonight.

Just Sheila and me stand, alone in the alley, the sun is setting on the other side of the building. Those sunset colors, red and yellow as a fire burning, on the other side of everywhere. Sheila's fingers flick the money back and forth between her hands, her mouth counting, ". . . fifty, seventy, a hundred twenty, a hundred seventy . . ." The money coming to $560 in her right hand. Then the same in her left.

Don't worry, I tell her. She can still hate her mom.

And Sheila counts the bills again, saying, "Thanks." She wipes her eyes with a twenty-dollar bill. She blows her nose on a fifty and says, "You smell meat cooking?"

I ask, is she going to poison me?

"Don't you know?" Sheila says, "The damaged love the damaged."

Cyanide and sugar. Poison and antidote. Like maybe we balance each other out.

I don't know. But this moment, standing with her in the alley, outside the stage door, the number "72" still going down my arm, waiting to do what's next, this moment feels like enough.

The ambulance guys still inside, chest-massaging the dead body of Mr. Bacardi. Sticking him with big needles full of some cure. His eyes squeezed shut from the huge smile his dead mouth is doing.

And Sheila says, "Wait." Half the money in each hand, she stops counting. She looks at the closed metal door we just came out. The door shut behind us. After the lock clicked, after everything's done. Sheila leans, twisting her head sideways until her ear presses to the door. She puts her nose to the lock and sniffs—her nostrils reaching for the keyhole and sniffing, hard. One hand, clenched full of money, reaches to tug the handle. Tugs harder. Her other hand, fisted around the other money, she knocks on the metal door. Knocks louder. Tugs harder. Sheila shoves both hands at me, saying, "Hold this crap a minute."

A little, little smell of meat smoke. Barbecue.

The red outline of my cross, the one pressed off my chest, fading on her cheek.

It's after she pushes all the cash into my hands Sheila starts really screaming, slapping and kicking the door, then tugging the handle with both hands.

34

Mr. 137

On the film set, the
emergency paramedics pound on the shaved chest of
Branch Bacardi, the latex of their gloves sticking, then
peeling off with a tearing sound, their latex palms
stained brown with bronzer, revealing Bacardi's dead
blue skin. Their hands punching and pumping Bacardi's chest, his red, dark-red nipple blood spots their
gloves. The razor cut, his shaved-off nipple no longer
leaking blood.

With the cameraman leaning close, the paramedics sweating, the sides of their shirts, from sleeve to
belt, their white uniforms soaked dark gray with sweat,
Cassie Wright says, "Are you getting this?" The production stills-photographer shooting coverage, flash after flash from every angle, washing everything in bursts
of strobe that leave us blind. Blinking. Breathing the
hot air, heavy with sweat and perfume and sperm.

At the same time, Cassie squats over Bacardi's hips,

sitting on the stubble of his shaved pubic hair. With both hands planted on her knees, she pushes down to raise herself. Half standing, she slams her hips down again, but not too fast, not so fast you can't see Bacardi's stiff blue erection disappearing inside her.

Even dead, that's a big dick.

The Goldilocks of dildos. Battery-powered or manually operated. Dead as the pink rubber version under my bed. As any holy relic in a cathedral. Stiff as the shrink-wrapped rows for sale in adult toy stores. Now a collectors' item. An antique.

Cassie Wright lifts her hips and slams them down, the flash of blue, lifeless dick appearing and disappearing, and she says, "Upstage me . . . you prick piece of shit." Both of them drenched in sweat. She pounds her pussy down, snarling, "You stole my biggest scene, you rat bastard." Her eyes washing tears down both cheeks, the runoff of eyeliner and mascara tracing the spidery wrinkles from her eyes to her chin, her face shattered by the network of branching black cracks.

One paramedic squeezes clear jelly from a tube, smears the jelly onto a little catcher's mitt. A small white mitt. Then the paramedic rubs the mitt against another little mitt, smearing the clear jelly between them. Wires dangle from both little mitts, trailing to a box where a red light glows.

The paramedic smearing jelly, he says, "Clear!"

The other paramedic leans back, away, not touching Bacardi.

The catcher's mitts, really cardiac paddles. A heart defibrillator. A billion volts of electricity, ready to shock Bacardi back to life.

The paramedic holding the cardiac paddles, he shouts, "Clear, lady!" into Cassie's broken, weeping face.

And Cassie stands until the fat blue erection is their only link. That dick their only connection. Until the fat head of it pops free of her dripping labia. The stiff blue dick still reaching out, stretching straight up to touch her as she pulls away.

The paramedic slams both cardiac paddles on Bacardi's sagging, sweating chest, and Bacardi's spine arcs from the current pumped into him. The muscles of his arms and legs swell, defined, etched and cut, his skin hard and tight. In that jolt, Bacardi looking young again, trim and tan, smooth and smiling. His teeth shining, white. His eyes shocked wide open. The photographer's flash and the spark of paramedic lightning turning Bacardi into a buff Frankenstein's monster.

And in that flash, Cassie Wright looks down at Branch Bacardi restored to his prime, young the way they'd both been young. His perfect comeback.

Could be it was suicide, could be her tired knees simply gave out.

The gesture was so *Romeo and Juliet.* But, wouldn't you know it . . .

It can only take a moment to waste the rest of your life.

With the billion volts of power still pulsing into Bacardi . . . the cameras rolling . . . Cassie Wright impales herself on his high-voltage, electric-chair, cattle-prod dick of death.

194

35

Sheila

Cardiac defibrillators set above 450 joules will leave contact burns. The paddles can scorch a patient's chest. Any metal jewelry can arc, blazing hot for an instant. Earrings or necklaces. On Branch Bacardi's sagging pecs, the two round red welts from the paddles could be cartoon nipples. Shiny new aureolas scarred into his chest. Ms. Wright's heart-shaped locket so hot it's burned into her chest. Branded Ms. Wright with a tiny heart. Both Bacardi's new nipples and Ms. Wright's heart still smoking. The locket's sprung open, the gold turned black, the baby picture, inside, curled and charred in a puff of smoke.

That picture of newborn baby me—a flash, a flame, and gone—burned to ash.

Staring down at Branch Bacardi, one paramedic wadwanker says, "Good thing, or there's no way we'd get a boner that big zipped inside any body bag."

195

"Forget that," says the other paramedic pud-puller. "That monster wouldn't fit inside a closed casket."

The defibrillator melted Bacardi and Ms. Wright into a human X. Joined at the hips. Their flesh married in hate, burned together deeper than any wedding could leave them. Conjoined. Cauterized.

But, no . . . they didn't die. Branch and Cassie. Almost, but not quite. The stench of scorched pussy and balls comes from the kilowatt jolt that almost killed Ms. Wright—but brought Branch Bacardi back to life. The shock that fused their genitals together. Sealed together.

True fact.

The paramedics just stare, shaking their heads over the problem of how to lift two unconscious bodies, Siamese twins bound by their groins, and haul them to the hospital. Seared together by a few layers of cooked skin, or a muscle spasm, or their soft parts baked into a shared meatloaf.

The smell of sweat and ozone and fried hamburger.

It's then I said it: Branch Bacardi and Cassie Wright are my father and mother. Are my parents. I'm their child.

True fact. Tapping myself on the chest, I tell the paramedics, "My name is Zelda Zonk."

But nobody looks up from the two naked bodies, both of them moaning, their heads lolling slack on their necks. Their eyes stay closed. Steam spiraling up from their fused flesh. Their new branding-iron nipples and heart.

With my fingers straight and held tight together, I raise one hand, the way you would for the Pledge of

Allegiance in school, for any promise to be sworn in court, and I give a little wave for the paramedics to look. With my other hand, I tap my chest. Tapping where my own heart's supposed to be.

For an instant, everything feels so important. Almost real.

And I say it again. My secret name. Raising my hand just a tiny bit higher, so someone might finally look and see me.

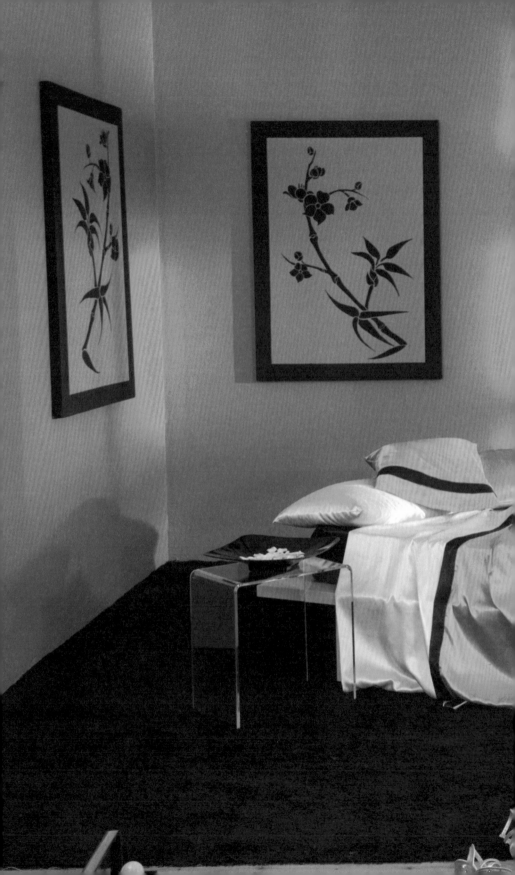